A FAMILY FOR THE AMISH ORPHANS

JO ANN BROWN

Recycling programs
for this product may
not exist in your area.

ISBN-13: 978-1-335-62167-2

A Family for the Amish Orphans

Love Inspired
22 Adelaide St. West, 41st Floor
Toronto, Ontario M5H 4E3, Canada
www.LoveInspired.com

HarperCollins Publishers
Macken House, 39/40 Mayor Street Upper,
Dublin 1, D01 C9W8, Ireland
www.HarperCollins.com

Printed in Lithuania

1 2 3 4 5 6 7 8 9 10 LIT 28 27 26 25

Two are better than one;
because they have a good reward for their labour.
For if they fall, the one will lift up his fellow:
but woe to him that is alone when he falleth;
for he hath not another to help him up.
—*Ecclesiastes* 4:9–10

Zvay zammah sinn bessah es aynah
veil si may greeya fa iahra eahvet;
Vann aynah anna fald kann da annah eem uf helfa
Avvah oahm is da mann es anna fald
un hott nimmand fa eem uf helfa!
—*Breddichah* 4:9–10

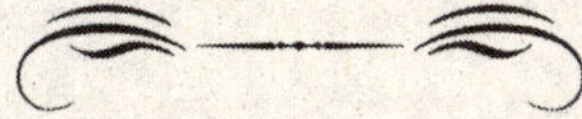

For Cherise Stalnecker
Thanks for making us look great...and your friendship!

"I didn't tell you everything that happened yesterday," Carrie said.

"What else?" Daryn braced himself, praying for the strength to accept what she had to tell him.

"Ella laughed, Daryn. Not a big laugh, but bigger than a snicker. A giggle."

He grasped her shoulders. "That's *wunderbaar*."

"It is. I'm sorry it took so long to tell you."

"*Danki* for letting me know." His fingers trailed across her shoulders, and her lips parted with a soft breath he heard more with his heart than his ears. He had had more to say, but the words vanished as he fell into her green eyes, which were as warm and welcoming as the spring sunshine.

Would she yank herself away if he pressed his lips to hers? Or would she kiss him? They hadn't had any time together as a couple should because they were always surrounded by others. Should he feel gratitude toward Carrie and nothing more?

His questions went unanswered as his nieces rushed toward them. A strange expression flashed across her face before she stepped away to greet the youngsters. Relief? Dismay? Uncertainty...?

Jo Ann Brown, a *New York Times* bestselling author, loves stories with happily-ever-after endings. A former military officer, she and her husband (her real hero who knows how to fix stubborn computer problems, especially when she's on deadline) live in Nevada with two spoiled cats and where they can usually be found showing off pictures of their twin grandsons. She loves hearing from readers. Drop her a note at joannbrownbooks.com.

Books by Jo Ann Brown

Love Inspired

Amish of Lost River

Healing Her Amish Heart
Saving Her Amish Baby
Their Amish Courtship Secret
A Family for the Amish Orphans

Amish of Prince Edward Island

Building Her Amish Dream
Snowbound Amish Christmas
Caring for Her Amish Neighbor
Unexpected Amish Protectors

Green Mountain Blessings

An Amish Christmas Promise
An Amish Easter Wish
An Amish Mother's Secret Past
An Amish Holiday Family

Visit the Author Profile page at LoveInspired.com for more titles.

Chapter One

"Want a drink."

"Want a pony ride."

Daryn Yutzy looked at the two little girls in the double stroller as they pointed at everything they passed in the park where food trucks had gathered to serve food to the crowds who'd finished viewing the Lost River Memorial Day parade fifteen minutes ago. His gaze slipped to five-year-old Ella whose fingers held the stroller's handle, but far enough away from his much bigger hand so there was no chance they'd touch.

"Want a flower."

"Want a swing."

He wanted something, too. A chance to look at the mountains surrounding the San Luis Valley in southern Colorado. Winter's snow clung to the highest peaks, but lower on the slopes, the trees were a lush green like the ones on the flat valley floor. It would have been great to drag in a single deep appreciative breath, flavored with the aromas of jalapeños and sausages and cotton candy. Most of all, he wanted a moment to get his head on straight. He hadn't had that since the three girls had arrived a week ago at Agua Estrella, the horse ranch where he worked about ten miles south of the small Colorado town of Lost River. Maybe if he'd had a second when he wasn't worried about making sure they ate and slept and had toys and weren't crying, he might find a way to persuade Ella to talk to him. Maybe he'd have time to eat and sleep himself and wouldn't be tempted to give into tears while he mourned the deaths of his sister, her husband and their son.

"Want pretty doll," continued the litany.

"Want *boppli* doll."

"Want *mamm* doll."

"Mamm!"

The younger two burst into tears. He offered eighteen-month-old Rachelle a sippy cup. She pushed it away and fought the straps in the double stroller while shrieking.

Heads turned from every direction, and he asked God, as he had so many other times since daybreak he'd lost count, for patience with his three nieces. Before last week, he'd known them through letters written by his older sister and sent from Missouri. Hope had adored her daughters and son, and each week, she'd shared their adventures with her brothers. That had ended with a horrific buggy accident. Daryn hadn't had a chance to deal with his grief before he learned, when a social worker came with three blond little girls, he'd been named their guardian.

Why him? His older brother was married and well-settled on a farm in the Canadian province of Prince Edward Island. He and his wife had a *boppli* and another on the way. Daryn was single and wasn't sure he planned to stay in the San Luis Valley. The social worker, a kind but harried woman, hadn't been able to tell Daryn anything except the couple's will had made him the guardian for their *kinder*.

Rachelle, who was very much a *boppli*, sat in one side of the stroller while her four-year-old sister Kayla perched on the edge of her seat. Their fine blond hair danced in the warm breeze that was too weak to dash away the tears rushing down their cheeks. Their older sister clutched the stroller's handle as if it were a lifeline, but he knew if he shifted his hand on the bar, she'd yank her fingers away and wrap her arms around herself.

He'd brought them to town because he'd hoped they'd enjoy the parade and the candy flung from the floats. The girls had watched in silence while other *kinder* ran to collect the treats. He was beginning to wonder if they were sleepwalking through their shock and grief.

As he was.

Daryn pulled three bananas from his backpack and offered them to his nieces. Rachelle took one and banged it against the stroller with another howl.

"Let me help," said a gentle voice from behind him.

He didn't dare take his eyes off the girls. Yesterday he had, and the youngest had ended up with scrapes on her chin from trying to climb onto the table. Before his exhausted brain could devise a response, a woman stepped around him.

He recognized her. Carrie Detweiler was the tallest woman in their plain community, but her green eyes were what always caught his attention. They were like a cat's eyes, cool and distant when she regarded him, though he'd noticed how they glowed with warmth for others. She didn't like him. That was okay, because he found her annoying with her constant smiles. Not that he'd given her much thought. He was too busy with ranch work and learning to raise bison.

And little girls.

God, why is it harder to know how to handle my nieces than a bison calf?

"Be careful," Carrie said as she squatted in front of the girls. "They're hot."

He realized she held a small container of French fries. Steam rose, and crystals of salt glittered on each fry. His stomach growled, and he recalled he'd missed breakfast while getting the girls ready.

The whole day had been a fiasco. He should have given up when he made the girls cry while trying to brush their hair. Braids took him too long, so they wore their hair in buns beneath netting his work-worn fingers snagged. He hadn't pulled the girls' hair, but the youngest had gotten bored of sitting while he tried to corral each silken strand while the oldest stormed away when he handed her a small mirror so she could see his efforts.

In spite of what he viewed as a valiant effort, the girls' hair hung along their chubby cheeks. He was sure he'd washed their faces before leaving the ranch. The only dirtier faces at the parade belonged to a pair of *Englisch* boys who must have been trespassing on the piles of dirt at the construction site a couple of blocks away. He'd seen glances in his direction, and he'd wanted to shout he was doing his best.

He knew his best had to get better. He couldn't shirk his obligation to his family.

Not again.

"Be careful. Blow on them." Carrie's lilting voice drew his attention to the present.

Because she squatted in front of the stroller as she drizzled ketchup on the fries, Daryn couldn't move it away with a mumbled excuse. Three sets of wide eyes were focused on the cardboard container. Her words of encouragement, gentle and soft, lured little fingers to stretch forward to take the fries.

"Be careful," she repeated. "Hot."

The aroma of the grease from the fries made him salivate. For a single second, his fingers moved to select one.

He pulled them back. The sooner he put an end to this, the better. He didn't need to add cheerful, always-smiling, not-a-care-in-the-world Carrie Detweiler to the mix of his already awful day.

His eyes narrowed. What was she wearing over her dark green dress? On top of her black apron was another unlike any he'd seen. It was black, too, but faint lines of white ran through the fabric. Across the bib were embroidered in white and green the words *Taters and Tales*. A series of big deep pockets had been sewn at the waist. Each one was big enough to hold the contents of his backpack. Were the pockets loaded with ketchup and salt packets?

Kayla and Rachelle were responding to her offer of food. He wasn't surprised when Ella snatched a single fry, then moved to keep the stroller between her and Carrie. And him, too, he realized because she stood on the opposite side.

The younger girls giggled, and Carrie's laugh underscored the sound. Daryn frowned. He could have done with less of Carrie's unending cheerfulness. Each time he'd seen her after church services, she'd been eager to make others laugh. She told silly stories and volunteered to organize games for the *kinder*. He'd heard she'd been an assistant teacher at the local school, and he could imagine her doing that. He wondered why she'd left to work in a diner.

"My name is Carrie," she was saying in her effervescent tone. "What's yours?" Her chuckle made her sound as young as the girls. "Sorry. I shouldn't have asked you a question when your mouths are full." She glanced at him with her intriguing eyes that were accented by the warm pink brushing her cheeks.

"The littlest one is Rachelle Byler," he said to answer her unspoken question. "She's my niece."

"Me Rae-Rae," chirped the toddler, surprising him because he hadn't known she had a nickname. What other things were the girls hiding from him? As the toddler licked salt off her fry, she said, "Yummy. More?"

Before Daryn could answer, Carrie held out two fries. Rachelle—Rae-Rae—grabbed both in her pudgy hands, squishing them into mush before jamming them into her mouth.

"The middle one is Kayla. She's four." He grimaced when he saw Kayla had ketchup across her face. He dug into his pocket for his handkerchief.

Carrie was faster than he was. She pulled a wet wipe from an oversized apron pocket and dabbed at Kayla's face. The little girl chortled. When Carrie handed her the damp square so she could clean her face herself, Kayla acted as if she'd been given a *wunderbaar* gift. She rubbed it along her cheeks, missing most places where ketchup clung. Looking up, she shook her head when Carrie asked if Kayla minded her cleaning the last few spots.

Carrie leaned forward and washed the four-year-old's face before offering her more fries and ketchup.

Daryn bit back his warning that it would become an unending cycle of cleaning, fries, cleaning and fries.

Not that he would have had time to say anything because Carrie was asking, "Who are you, pumpkin?"

"She's Ella. She's the oldest. She's five years old," Daryn said, knowing Ella wouldn't talk to Carrie. She hadn't spoken a single word in the past week. The social worker had said Ella might require special help to get over her loss.

He hadn't asked what the social worker meant. There had been too many questions he'd failed to pose while his brain reeled with the shock of having three small girls he'd never met put into his care.

"More fries, Ella?" Carrie asked.

Daryn was astonished when the little girl snagged several. So astonished, he said, "Tell Carrie *danki* for the fries, Ella."

When the little girl continued to stare at the strips in her hand and was silent, he wanted to kick himself. Why was he asking Ella to talk to Carrie when he hadn't heard a sound from her? Maybe Ella had talked to her sisters since they came to Agua Estrella. If so, he'd missed it. Not knowing what Ella's voice sounded like was beginning to creep him out, but every effort he'd made to convince her to talk had been futile.

"Want some, Daryn?" Carrie asked as she came to her feet and offered him the half-filled container.

He was tall for an Amish man, but her eyes were even with his. It had startled him on the few occasions—very few—when he'd let himself get maneuvered into standing close to her.

Dropping his gaze to the fries, he took a handful as if he hadn't had a decent meal in months. That was close to the truth. Though the Marquezes, who owned the ranch where he worked, had invited him to move from the bunkhouse into a small house behind their home the day the girls arrived, he'd been collecting food from the ranch cook and bringing it to the log cabin each night. That meant beans and hot dogs and not much else. The aroma of the Hispanic food from the main house made his mouth water, but the cook in the bunkhouse cooked what he deemed "cowboy food." Once in a while, chili was served, but it didn't have any heat. Just tomato sauce, meat and beans.

Daryn needed to learn to make meals for his nieces, but grilled cheese or peanut butter sandwiches were the extent of his culinary talent. Such a diet wouldn't be *gut* for growing *kinder*.

Taking a bite of the fries, his eyes widened. "These are amazing! Where did you get them?"

"From my food trailer." She held up the last of the fries. "Want to finish them off?"

He wished he and the girls could have food this *gut* every day, but the last thing he needed in his life was another female upsetting his routine. *Please, God, no more females intruding on my life.* It was a ridiculous prayer but it came from the depths of his heart.

"I didn't know you could cook," he said as he scooped up the remaining fries, leaving small scraps on the bottom of the container. They were his favorite, but he didn't know how to pick them up without tilting the cardboard toward him. The motion seemed too greedy. "I thought you were just a waitress."

When strong emotion flashed in her eyes, he regretted the words. He should apologize, blaming his exhaustion and stress. She didn't give him a chance, bending over the stroller to offer the scraps to the youngsters. Her motion made it clear his insult had been worse than he'd guessed.

Another horrible thing on a horrible day. *It's got to get better, God, ain't so?*

Not for the first time in his life, he feared the answer would be no.

Carrie Detweiler didn't let her smile slip as she held out the scraps to the two little girls in the stroller before motioning for Ella to help herself. She doubted the *kinder* had seen a smile since their arrival in Lost River. Though she hadn't felt much like smiling since her sister had jumped the fence almost two years ago, she'd made it a habit. Dumping her grief on others was cruel, so it was better to wear a happy mask that put others at ease.

Daryn Yutzy didn't seem to feel the same. He was a *gut-*looking man with his hair that was a combination of light brown and sun-bleached white. He had a strong jaw. Today, it was wreathed with pale stubble highlighting its stubborn lines. His eyes were as blue as a summer sky, but he was too serious. When others told jokes, he didn't crack a smile.

He'd moved to Lost River last year and taken a job at Agua Estrella, the Marquezes' ranch, working with horses. He avoided youth gatherings. As soon as he could politely do so, he left whichever house was hosting church. If he did anything for fun, she hadn't heard about it.

Her twin sister, Bethany, would have fallen hard for him, as she had for any guy with a hard jaw and an intense gaze. Bethany had been in love every day since she was twelve, but seldom two days in a row with the same boy. Had that changed when her sister left Lost River and her family?

The all-too-familiar sorrow cut through Carrie. When Bethany vanished two years ago, emptiness had torn apart Carrie's heart. It was as if she'd mislaid a part of herself as vital as her hands and feet. Carrie had spent the time trying to ease her parents' dismay while moving *her* life forward the best she could. That meant chasing her dream of having her own business. If she kept busy, she wouldn't have time to think. In addition, she could earn money to help her learn where Bethany was now.

In the meantime, she wasn't going to act like Daryn. Nobody seemed to know why he was always glum. Maybe that was how God had made him. If so, she pitied him. Having a chuckle with friends or smiling when a spring morning was glorious with sunshine and wild flowers after the hard Colorado winter were experiences she wouldn't want to miss.

She chided herself. The most joy-filled person would have been sad after learning of his family's deaths. Though the accident had taken place in Missouri, it had been the topic of conversation for two full days at the diner where she worked as a waitress most mornings. Learning young *kinder* had been left without parents augmented the tragedy.

"Daryn, I was so sorry to hear about—"

He waved her to silence. "Little ears."

She nodded, berating herself for being insensitive. Her smile returned when Rae-Rae gazed at her and asked, "More?"

"Later. Okay? I need to get to my food trailer." She pointed to the green-and-white box on wheels which she'd rehabbed over the winter. Today's event was her third. For a second, she felt she was running away from the disquieting sight of three beautiful little girls who were orphans. She shook that thought away as Daryn spoke.

"*Ja.* You've got customers waiting." His voice was flat, and she almost asked if he could read her thoughts.

"I'll be right there!" she called with a wave.

When the people waiting by the order window waved back, her smile became genuine. The burgeoning business was growing faster than she'd dared to hope. The variety of food she offered wasn't broad yet, but she had ideas she couldn't wait to add to her menu.

"Before I go," she asked, "would you like books, girls?"

When their eyes got wide as the younger ones nodded, she fought to keep her smile in place. Ella continued to stare at the stroller's wheels.

Poor little girl. Carrie wanted to sweep her into her arms and reassure her everything would be okay. How could she when it wasn't the truth? They'd lost so much.

Carrie understood that too well, because there were days when she wanted to crawl into a hole and draw it in after her. She struggled with her grief at Bethany's leaving by trying to lose herself in her new business, which combined her three favorite things: cooking, interacting with the public and sharing her love of reading. She collected used children's books from thrift shops and church rummage sales and friends. With her apron's big pockets filled with books from the box she kept in the trailer, she was ready when she saw a *kind* looking at the trio of books she kept between wooden apple bookends on the trailer's serving counter. The *kinder* were thrilled with the unexpected gift, and she hoped it might be the book that triggered a love for reading.

She dug into her pockets and pulled out three books. One was a board book with a pair of bears on the cover. She handed it to Rae-Rae and then gave Kayla a picture book about a kitten with big bright eyes. The final one was a small edition of a favorite fairy tale. She offered it to Ella but the *kind* didn't take it.

"This is a story about a girl who's got the same name you do. Ella," Carrie said. "Though her step*mamm* calls her Cinderella."

"What's a step*mamm*?" asked Kayla, who was half standing in the stroller to see the cover decorated with a castle and glass slipper.

Seeing Daryn's face turn gray beneath his deep tan, Carrie wished she'd chosen a different book. In her enthusiasm to share her love of books, she'd let herself forget how sad many fairy tales were. Missing parents, abandoned *kinder*, broken hearts of every sort.

Somehow she managed to say, "It's a different kind of *mamm*, but the story is really about a prince and a castle and a special shoe."

Kayla looked at her black sneakers. "I like shoes."

"*Gut.*" She needed to make her escape before she was

overwhelmed by sympathy for Daryn, who must face this barrage every day.

As she took a single step toward her trailer, shoving the copy of *Cinderella* into a pocket, her way was blocked by a broad chest in a light blue shirt and black suspenders. She raised her eyes toward Daryn's, an odd experience because she was accustomed to being the tallest in most groups.

"*Danki* for giving the girls the fries…" He swallowed hard before adding, "And the books."

She must apologize. "I'm sorry about choosing that book. I thought about how the girl was called Ella, too. If it makes things more difficult for you—"

"Nothing can make anything *more* difficult."

"How are they doing?"

"I don't know. We don't talk about their lives in Missouri or their parents or brother." He glanced at the girls. The ones in the stroller were paging through their books while Ella watched them with no expression. "Eli was Ella's twin."

Pain welled in his eyes. She almost put her hand on his arm to let him know it was okay to show strong emotions. In fact, she'd been told by their bishop it was important not to suppress pain and joy. Each was a gift from God, a way of bringing her closer to her Heavenly *Daed*, who celebrated and mourned, too.

From the first time she'd seen Daryn during a church service after he'd joined their community, he'd kept her at arm's length. Others returned her smiles. From him, she'd seen frowns and disapproval. She wasn't sure what he disapproved of, though she suspected he considered her frivolous.

"Poor little one," she said with a sigh. "I know what it's like to lose a twin."

"Your sister—"

"Is gone, Daryn." She couldn't keep frustration from her

voice. Not with him, but with the people who'd believed she should be grateful her sister might return.

She would have said more but a tiny hand tugged on her apron, and she was glad for the excuse to look away from his taut face.

"I'll bring fries when—" The rest of her words clogged in her throat when she realized it was Daryn's oldest niece by her side. "I'll get you fries in a minute, Ella. Okay?"

"Book," Ella said in a soft whisper as she reached for it.

Grabbing the book out of her pocket, she gave it to the little girl. "Enjoy reading about another Ella."

The *kind* nodded and turned away, pressing the book close to her chest as if she feared it'd be snatched away.

Tears rose in Carrie's eyes. Why shouldn't Ella feel that way? Her precious *mamm* and *daed* and twin brother had been taken without warning. How well did the girls know Daryn? Word around the community was he had wandering feet, having lived in various places before coming to Colorado.

Daryn gasped. "Carrie, how did you do that?"

"Do what?"

"Tell me how you got Ella to talk. I've got to know. Help me, Carrie!"

Chapter Two

Daryn recoiled when he heard Carrie's gasp. Was he out of his mind? He already had three females in his life, altering it in ways he couldn't have imagined last month. He'd believed he didn't need another.

But he did. At least for as long as it took for Carrie to explain how she'd done what she'd done.

Somehow, and he had no idea how, Carrie had persuaded Ella to speak. A single word, it was true, but one more than he'd managed to get from the little girl. He searched Carrie's face, seeking an answer. What special words had she said? What gesture had she made to reach past Ella's wall of silent grief? What had created a connection between the two of them? Would it last long enough to help him ease the little girl into her new life?

How amazing that Carrie had reached Ella! Everything he'd tried in the past week had been for naught. Friends had tried to break through to the little girl, too. If two former schoolteachers and a variety of loving *mamms* hadn't succeeded, how had Carrie?

"Daryn, I've got customers waiting." Carrie's voice had taken on a sharp edge he'd never heard her use. Though he had to admit, he'd talked to her more today than any other time. Her unending cheerful outlook could become tiresome for a man who had important matters to consider.

He'd surprised himself as much as he had her when he grasped her arm to keep her there. She froze. When he leaned toward her, she edged away as far as she could.

"How did you do it?" he whispered, not wanting the little girls to overhear. "How did you convince her to talk to you?"

"I don't know why she spoke to me." Carrie eased herself from his grip.

"Hey, Carrie!" came a shout from the long line by the food truck. "Are you open for business, or are you going to leave us to starve?"

When laughs burst from the people queued up, Daryn realized he'd recognized the voice. It belonged to his friend, Kolton Lehman, who was teaching him the ins and outs of building a bison herd. Since Kolton had had a successful calving season at the same time he found an unexpected family, the herdsman had seldom been without a grin and a jest.

"I've got to go," Carrie said.

The words hung in the invisible lines of tension between them, then vanished as she ran to the truck, which looked as if it had been built as a travel trailer seventy-five years before. He heard a door slam, and then she was standing in the window under the awning. She talked to her customers as she prepared food and served it. Every person walked away with a happy expression.

Daryn looked at his nieces. Rae-Rae's head was nodding, and Kayla had fallen asleep. Ella remained awake and stood like a sentry behind the stroller, the book held close to her.

"Would you like me to read you that story when we get home?" he asked.

The wrong question, because when he said the word

home, tears hung on her lashes. What a *dummkopf* he was! Why would Ella consider where they lived home? For her, home was in Missouri with her whole family. Her lower lip began to wobble.

"Hungry?" he asked to forestall any tears, though he hadn't seen Ella cry. Her sisters had. A lot.

Rae-Rae sat straighter. "Fries!"

"How about something different? Tacos would be *gut*, ain't so?"

"Want fries!" The toddler banged her fists on the stroller.

Kayla woke with a start, rubbing her eyes, "Want fries."

Knowing he'd be smart to concede before the request became a demand that drew more attention to them, he said, "All right. Let's get some fries."

He pushed the stroller to the end of the line, hoping the girls would be patient. It helped that the younger two fell asleep while he walked forward as each customer was served. Beside him, Ella was silent. When other kids ran past, calling to her to join in their game, she remained mute.

"What can I get for you?" Carrie asked as she folded her arms on the counter under the white-and-black-striped awning decorated with the words *Taters and Tales*. The green paint on the sides was a shade darker than her eyes. "You can see what my food trailer offers on the board to your right above the books."

The sign with a list of quick-serve foods was decorated with book covers. Most of the titles he'd read when he first went to school. He'd been an eager reader before he'd traded the adventures in them for trying to find his own…and ending up in trouble.

Pushing that thought aside, Daryn said, "I thought these were called food trucks."

"They are when they've got a motorized section." She

wiggled her fingers, and he heard the younger girls giggling behind him. They must be awake. "Greenie Gal is a trailer. A friend uses her truck to move it for me."

"You named your food trailer?"

"Why not? Didn't God have Adam name all the creatures on the earth?"

"Creatures, *ja*, but a trailer?" He shook his head. Giving the garish trailer a name wasn't what he needed to talk to her about.

"What can I get you?"

Grateful for the opening she'd given him, he said, "Right now, fries for the girls. Later, your time."

Her golden brows lowered. "For what?"

"Fries first."

Her gaze scanned his face and then, her smile fading, she nodded. She turned from the window. When she looked at him, she held three containers of fries. She put them below the counter before he could take them.

"*Komm* around to the back," she said. "They can eat there without your worrying they'll get trampled."

He complied, lifting the stroller over the thick wires powering the trucks. Seeing a bench behind the trailer, he motioned for Ella to sit as the door opened.

Carrie was smiling as she placed a napkin on each girl's lap before putting a container of fries on top of it. "You'll have to sit still so you don't spill."

"Eat them!" Kayla announced.

"That's another way to make sure they don't spill." Carrie chuckled as she offered the last container to Ella. "You can put the book on the bench, if you'd like."

Ella did, then reached for the container.

"Let me." Carrie spread a napkin across the girl's knees. When Ella squirmed and giggled, Carrie asked, "Ticklish?"

Daryn watched in disbelief as Ella gave her a fleeting smile and murmured, "*Ja.*"

How had Carrie done it? How had she persuaded Ella to talk and laugh and smile? He had to know.

God, give me the right words.

"Carrie?" he asked, motioning for her to move a short distance from the girls to where the noise from the crowd would swallow their words. "Will you spend time with Ella?"

"Just Ella?"

"With Kayla and Rach—with Rae-Rae, too." He sighed. "I thought I'd be too pushy if I'd asked about all three."

"They're close to each other."

"*Ja,* but you've broken through to them as I haven't been able to. Will you help me?"

Carrie didn't answer right away, and his heart plummeted to the depths of despair and grief. Didn't she see how desperate he was? He was asking for her help, in spite of the fact nobody could describe them as friends.

"Carrie, talking to the kids is like trying to tiptoe through a raging flood. On every step, I could put my foot in the wrong place and drop into the deep end." He sighed. "Or put my foot in my mouth like now."

"It's okay. I know you're worried about them. Everyone is."

"Will you help by spending time with them?"

"*Ja.*" She held up her hand to halt his reply. "I will when I can. I've got my job at the diner as well as Greenie Gal."

"I'm not looking for a babysitter."

"*Gut,* because I—"

"Carrie Detweiler, where are you?" came an angry shout from the other side of the trailer that turned them, including the *kinder*, into statues.

At the same time, a surprising sensation rushed through

him as he found himself ready to protect her as well as his nieces. He needed to regain his equilibrium.

Fast.

Seeing Daryn's shoulders stiffen, Carrie forced hers to relax. Finding her smile was difficult, but she did. She managed a laugh and a wink for the three little girls. It must have been enough because they returned to their fries.

"It's okay," she said before facing her brother, who was storming around the trailer.

When Gerald's eyes narrowed, she wanted to roll hers. Her brother, who was a half head taller than she was, had broad shoulders that had convinced more than one man— or so she'd heard along the Amish grapevine—it was a *gut* idea not to learn if Gerald could be goaded to set aside his pacifist ways. A single blow with one of his great fists could have done a lot of damage.

"Gerald, I didn't expect to see you here," she said when her brother stamped toward them as if trying to set off an earthquake.

She wasn't being honest. She should have known her brother would appear if she spoke to an unmarried man. If she hadn't been so caught up in the discussion about Daryn's nieces, she would have been shocked Gerald hadn't already tried to put a stop to their conversation. She'd tried to convince her brother not to loiter near the serving counter. She'd reminded him that he was tall, and if he stood too close, he blocked her menu. That could prevent customers from seeing it, and his grim expression would cost her potential customers.

She watched the two men appraise each other, and she couldn't help wondering what they were thinking. No, she didn't have to wonder what was in Gerald's mind. He'd be anxious to know what Daryn's intentions were. After Bethany had jumped the fence, her family had been determined Carrie not follow. Carrie told Gerald she had no interest in a relationship, but he didn't believe her. She'd almost told him about her plans to earn money with Greenie Gal to hire a private detective to find Bethany. She hadn't, uncertain how he'd react.

Gerald's eyes widened when his gaze alighted on the girls, then his brow furrowed. He shot a frown at them. All three ignored him as they concentrated on their fries.

Carrie didn't let her smile waver. Silencing her amused question of why he was trying to intimidate preschoolers, she said, "The day is going well, ain't so? I hadn't guessed we'd have such a big turnout."

"*Ja.* Seems like everyone and their *brother* is here." His frown was aimed at Daryn.

"I'm their *onkel*," Daryn replied, not letting her brother daunt him.

Gerald sputtered, and she guessed he hadn't thought Daryn would be calm. Respect for Daryn came to life inside her.

Not waiting for Gerald to retort, Carrie said, "I'll do what I can to help, Daryn. I'll get the rest of the week's schedule tomorrow at the diner. I'll know more then."

"Sounds *gut*." Without another word, he walked to the stroller, collected the *kinder* and, with Ella following as she balanced her fries and her book, left.

"I don't like him hanging around here," Gerald said.

"Nobody's hanging around here. Folks are here to sample the food and celebrate the holiday." She reached for the trailer's rear door. "I've got to get to work."

Her hope that Gerald would take her hint was dashed when he followed her. The space was cramped with a pair of deep fryers and a griddle. Every inch was filled with equipment and supplies, even the spot where she'd planned to put an oven. She wasn't a great baker, but Bethany was, and when Carrie had conceived of having a food trailer, she'd envisioned her sister as part of it.

Everything had been turned upside down when Bethany left one night without a note. Carrie had known her sister had been mooning over a guy, rumor suggested, she'd met at the ice cream shop. An *Englischer*. The plans Carrie had made for her life with her twin had fallen apart when she woke to find Bethany's bed not slept in and her personal items gone. Not her clothes, but her favorite teddy bear and the quilt their *grossmammi* had made when they were born. Carrie had been shocked when her sister took what had belonged to both of them, but she hoped it was keeping her sister warm and comforted.

She tried to ignore her brother as she filled orders. It wasn't easy. She kept elbowing him aside as she moved from one side of the trailer to the other. He didn't leave even when it was time to close. She began to clear the serving area, then dropped the awning. A glance at the clock over the storage area told her she had an hour to clean up and stow everything before moving the trailer to the farm.

"Here!" She shoved a big box of napkins into Gerald's arms. "Make yourself useful. Put that behind the top door."

"Is that what Daryn is looking to do? Be useful?"

With a sigh, she replied, "Gerald, you need to stop looking for trouble when there isn't any."

"Funny you should mention trouble." He shoved the box into its compartment and shut the door. "There are stories about the trouble Daryn has gotten himself into from when he was a kid."

"Most of us get into trouble at one time or another when

we're young." It felt odd to defend a man she didn't like, but she kept seeing the sad smiles on his nieces' faces as they tried to be happy.

"From what I've heard, that trouble was going on right up until he left Wyoming and came here. It's not like trouble follows him. He was right at the epicenter."

As she kept cleaning her equipment and giving him things to store, she said, "I don't like gossip. It's too mean-spirited. Remember the verse *Daed* read last night from the Book of James? 'Speak not evil one of another, brethren.'"

"The truth isn't evil."

She arched her brows. "No, truth isn't evil, but gossip can be hurtful." Switching off the griddle, she got a cloth to wipe the surfaces around it.

"Okay. Do you want to hear the truth about Daryn Yutzy?"

Facing him, she shook her head. "No."

"Because you're in love with him?"

A laugh burst from her. "Quite the opposite. His company is so depressing I try to avoid him." She glanced toward the service window as if she could see through it. "He cares a lot about his nieces, I've got to say."

Gerald pounced on her words. "What makes you think he isn't looking for a *mamm* for those kids?" His gray-green eyes narrowed. "If he ropes you into marrying him by making you feel those kids need a new *mamm*, you know what will happen next."

"No, I don't know because it isn't going to happen." She didn't add how spending time with Daryn's nieces reminded her of when she and Bethany were young and played to-gether. Instead, she patted the stainless steel counter. "I've got to make Greenie Gal a success, so I can pay the loan I took to buy it and fix it up. Including the one-hundred-and-fifty dollars you lent me." She tried to smile, but guessed it looked grotesque. It felt that way.

She was grateful to Gerald for offering the last money she needed to buy a battered trailer and his help in turning it into a portable kitchen where she could cook fries and burgers and other handheld sandwiches. However she wished he'd accept that though she and Bethany were identical in appearance, although Bethany was six inches shorter than Carrie, they were different in personalities and hopes and dreams.

As if she'd voiced her thoughts, he said, "You're not going to make the same mistake Bethany did, Carrie. I vowed before God I won't let that happen."

Again she yearned to roll her eyes, but didn't. If there was anyone in their family like Bethany, it was Gerald. Bethany had been distraught each time a boy she walked out with asked to drive another girl home. The house had been filled with Bethany's melodramatic tears and heavy steps as she carried the burden of what she saw as treachery…until she found another guy she thought might be "the one." Gerald was being just as dramatic. Vows before God? She bit back her laugh because she knew he'd be hurt by what he saw as her belittling him.

"Gerald," she said, glad her voice sounded sincere as she held his gaze, "I appreciate how much you care, but you've got to trust me." How she wished she could explain to him why she'd bought the trailer and redone it! If he had any idea she was putting aside money in order to hire a private detective to find their sister, he might run to the bishop with that information.

Would Jerek Stahl, their bishop, put a stop to her plan? He was forward-thinking, but having one of the *Leit* hiring an *Englischer* to trace her twin sister could prove to be a step too far. The community depended on him to deal with law enforcement. When her friend, Ruthie, had been offered a position as a native interpreter for the county court, she'd sought his approval and blessing before embarking on the training. Going behind his back as well as the full community's and her family's to retain an investigator might prove to be the biggest mistake she'd ever made.

She would risk that.

"I thought I could trust Bethany," Gerald replied. "She betrayed us."

"I can't believe she saw leaving that way. She must have been sure following her heart was the route God intended for her to take."

"She was mistaken." He wagged a finger in front of her face. "Like you'll be if you let Daryn Yutzy drag you into whatever mess he's sure to cause here. Do you hear me?"

"*Ja.*" She heard the hurt that was laced through his warning. Though she'd known her brother and her parents were suffering as much as she was from losing her twin, it was always painful to be reminded of it. She wished they could sit and pray together, but instead *Daed* and *Mamm* seldom spoke of their missing daughter. At the same time, they and Gerald had closed around Carrie so tightly she found it tough to breathe, let alone follow her plan to learn the truth about why Bethany had left.

Had her sister been pregnant as whispers suggested? Had she gone of her own free will? Where was she?

And the question that haunted Carrie the most: Did Bethany miss Carrie as much as Carrie missed her?

Chapter Three

The bell over the door at the Central Valley Diner rang when Daryn walked in the next day. It was the middle of the morning, and the early risers had eaten and gone off to work while the lunch crowd wouldn't begin trickling in for at least another hour. Scanning the space that would have made Elvis feel at home, he saw Carrie by a beverage dispenser behind the long stainless steel and white counter. Her back was to him as she put glasses from the dishwasher onto a shelf next to the window where finished food would be set.

Her blond hair was brushed beneath her *kapp*. Instead of her usual black apron, she wore a white one around her waist, accenting her slender profile, which had been hidden beneath her bulky apron with the huge pockets. Light caressed her hair with gold, and his fingers tingled as he imagined stroking it.

Have you lost every bit of your mind? He gritted his teeth, furious with his reaction to her. If he'd been looking to build a relationship before the girls arrived—which he hadn't been—he wasn't now. Carrie Detweiler wouldn't have been on his relationship radar anyhow. Everything about her was silly from her grin to the name of her food truck—no, make that food *trailer*—to her apron with its giant pockets.

Yet, she somehow had made a connection with Ella and

had said she'd help him do the same. For his niece, he'd put up with Carrie's odd ways. That's why he'd accepted *Doktor* Lynny's offer to watch the girls while he came to the diner. The veterinarian was married to his boss and lived in the big house in front of the cabin they'd given him after his nieces arrived.

Daryn strode past well-worn tables where paper mats covered dings and gouges left from decades of customers. He paid no attention to the jukebox that blinked bright lights in a vain attempt to convince him to put in a few coins. He didn't speak as he headed toward one of the chrome stools. It was easy to imagine his nieces swiveling on them. Kayla and Rae-Rae would love them. He had no idea what Ella liked except for the book Carrie had given her. She'd taken it to bed with her last night and brought it to the table during breakfast, protecting it when Kayla splashed *millich* on the table.

A motion caught his eye, and he noticed a man slouching in one of the red vinyl booths. Was it Carrie's brother Gerald, keeping an eye on her as usual? It wasn't. The man—and on second glance, teen was the appropriate term—was as tall as a Detweiler and had the same blond hair, but he wore black-rimmed glasses. His clothes looked as messy as Daryn's nieces', and Daryn wondered if the kid had been traveling too. If so, how had he gotten to the diner? The parking lot was empty, and it wasn't an easy walk along the main road from Lost River to Alamosa because traffic moved at top speed.

He gave the teen a nod, but was ignored. Standard adolescent attitude, he decided, glad he didn't have to deal with the kid. He could hear his *daed*'s laugh echoing in his head.

"What goes around comes around," *Daed* had repeated

on a regular basis once Daryn became a teenager. "I hope God blesses you with a boy just like you."

Sneering and walking away in a huff had been Daryn's response. It hadn't been his finest hour.

Or his worst.

Taking off his black cowboy hat, he slapped it against his broadfall black denim trousers. He'd given up wearing his plain straw hat while working with animals, because the only way to keep it on was to add an elastic chin strap like toddlers wore.

The sound of his boot heels on the black-and-white square tiles must have alerted her because Carrie turned with a smile. It faded when her gaze met his, but she raised her chin. Could it be that she didn't like him any more than he liked her? The sobering thought should have been a relief after the mess a woman had made of his life in Wyoming before he moved to Colorado. It would have been if he hadn't been fascinated moments ago by the sunshine glow on her hair.

Remember why you're here. The stern warning rang through his head in his *daed*'s voice. Not that his *daed* had spoken those exact words before he had grown too aggravated with Daryn's immature antics and sent him to live with his older brother in Prince Edward Island, hoping Daryn would change.

He hadn't.

Pushing aside the past because all it could do was make him more miserable, Daryn straddled a stool as if it were a horse. He folded his arms on the counter and asked, "Do you know your work schedule for this week?"

"Well, hello to you, too." She lifted the *kaffi* pot off its stand. "Want some?"

"*Ja*." As he watched her pour it, he said, "To the top. I'm drinking it black today."

"All right." She pulled the pot away with a flourish that prevented a drop from hitting the counter. Looking over his shoulder, she asked, "Want a cup, Perry?"

The teen mumbled an answer. With a shrug, she set the pot in its place.

"You understood what he said?" Daryn picked up his cup and took a careful sip. He fought not to grimace, but the *kaffi* was bitter without the usual cream he put in it.

She shook her head. "I don't speak teenager any longer, but if he wants something, he'll let me know." Raising her voice, she called, "Don't forget to take the trash out."

There came a mumble, but the lanky teen stood and shambled over to the container by the door. He took the top off and lifted out the bag. With the same shuffling steps, as if his feet were too heavy to lift, he walked past the counter and toward the back door.

"New hire?" Daryn asked.

"No, my cousin."

"Is he visiting?"

"You could say that. His parents have thrown up their hands in despair at his refusal to listen to them. They've shipped him here, hoping hard work will straighten him up."

"Sitting in a diner isn't hard work." Daryn's tone was gruff, but he wondered if Perry had been involved in as much mischief as he had. Abrupt sympathy roiled through him, because he knew how angry and alone the kid was feeling.

"If you'd been listening to him complain for the past two hours, you'd think being here was one of Job's trials. My folks wanted to give him time to adjust after his trip from Delaware."

"And your brother saw this as a chance for someone else to keep a close eye on you."

She laughed, but the sound had an edge. "You're getting it." Picking up a cloth, she swept it over the counter that appeared pristine to him. "I do have my schedule for the week, Daryn, but Perry's arrival has put a wrench in the works."

"Ella has reverted to silence after speaking to you. If she remains mute, I'll have to talk to the bishop about getting her help."

"That might be necessary. If—"

A crash and raised voices came from the rear of the diner.

Daryn passed Carrie as she raced through the kitchen. Pulling open the door, he faltered when he saw two people wrestling in the dirt. He winced when he heard flesh strike bone.

Carrie tried to shove past him. He pushed her into the doorway as he used the roar he reserved for getting a bunch of recalcitrant cows moving. Grabbing the boy on top by his shirt, he lifted him off. Perry was on the bottom and had taken the worst of the beating. Shoving the other boy against the diner's wall, Daryn glowered at both of them.

"Get up!" he snapped at Perry.

The boy did, wiping blood from his nose before he pushed his glasses back into place. Carrie thrust a handful of paper towels in his direction, then offered some to the other boy, an *Englischer* Daryn realized for the first time.

"Who are you?" Daryn asked.

The boy clamped his lips closed.

"You can let him go," Carrie said. "That's Bradley Monte. His *grossmammi* owns the diner." She glanced from one teen to the other. "Why are you two fighting?"

Bradley spat, then said, "He didn't fight. He tried to run away with whatever he was trying to steal." He pointed to the bag on the ground. Used napkins and straws were scattered beside it. Defiant, the teen snarled, "Some people will steal anything."

"He wasn't stealing." Daryn released the *Englisch* boy. "He was taking out the trash."

"How was I supposed to know that?"

"You could have asked," fired back Perry.

"Enough!" Daryn motioned both boys to pick up the trash before the wind sent it across the empty fields. Once they'd complied, he said, "Inside."

Carrie was upset he guessed by how she was wringing her hands in her small apron. A thought of comforting her fled through his head, but he shoved it aside. Instead he turned to Perry as the teen was about to walk past him.

"You did well by not raising your fists to him," Daryn said, lifting his hand to clap the boy on the back.

Perry sidestepped and, hanging his head, hurried into the diner. With a snicker that made Perry's shoulders stiffen, Bradley followed.

"I'll find something to keep them busy," Carrie said. "Busy and apart. His *grossmammi* usually gives me a heads-up when Bradley's coming to the diner. She must have forgotten." She sighed. "I know she's been having a tough time with him."

"Like your cousin?"

"They've got more in common than they can guess."

"It won't be easy. Boys don't always go looking for trouble, but it finds them." *As it finds me.*

She whirled to face him. "You sound like you know something about handling boys like them. Will you help me with Perry? Talk to him, spend time with him, help get him settled."

"Your brother should be the one to help him."

"Perry doesn't like Gerald. Never has. Thinks he's too nosy and bossy." She chuckled. "I agree, but that doesn't change the fact Perry needs someone. Will you help him?"

Was God laughing at him? He'd prayed for no more females in his life, and God had sent a stubborn, angry teenage boy. "Carrie, I—"

"Don't tell me you've got too much to do." She wagged a finger at him. "You wouldn't take no for an answer when you asked me to spend time with your nieces and I told you all I had to do. I'm not going to take no from you."

"I've got three little girls to watch." He glanced at the clock over the sink.

"I know you're busy, but so am I. My cousin needs help adjusting as the girls do. Let's help each other."

It made perfect sense, but Daryn had discovered no plans he made ended up close to perfect. However, he needed her help, so what choice did he have?

"How do you want this to work?" he asked.

"Let's discuss it over a cup of *kaffi* after I find something to keep the boys busy." She glanced at the stainless steel panels behind the griddle. Grease had splattered spots across it. "Cleaning that will keep one busy."

He pointed to the three-door refrigerator next to him. "There are a lot of fingerprints on these doors. Getting rid of them will occupy the other one."

She smiled. "See? You're helping already. This is going to work great."

He hoped those weren't famous last words.

Carrie heard the anguished cries from inside the small log cabin on the Agua Estrella Ranch as she walked up the steps that evening, toting three insulated bags along with her purse whose strap threatened to fall off her shoulder with each motion. The house was a miniature version of the great house where the owners lived. She knew the inside because her friend Mollie's husband had lived there with his two *kinder* when he first came to work in the San Luis Valley. It was comfortable and cozy and would have everything Daryn needed to make a home for his nieces.

Except someone—or maybe a couple of someones—wasn't happy.

Knocking on the door, she waited on the porch. She smiled when it opened, and Daryn peered out.

He *was* a handsome man, though not when he had what appeared to be peanut butter on his blond hair. The short golden whiskers had returned, but they couldn't pull her eyes from his grateful expression.

"Carrie! You're a sight for sore eyes." He reached up to touch the mess in his hair. "They're wound up. I can handle one or two, but they're all refusing to eat."

"What are you feeding them?"

He stepped onto the porch, leaving the door ajar. "I'd planned on peanut butter sandwiches tonight."

"Peanut butter? Hmm, I can see that." She was curious how it had gotten in his hair. "They don't like it?"

"They loved it this morning and at lunch."

She shook her head in astonishment. "They don't want the same food for every meal."

"I eat peanut butter all the time."

Raising her eyes toward the heavens, she prayed for serenity and the right words to reach this overwhelmed man. He'd been able, she'd heard, to help birth Kolton Lehman's bison calves earlier in the spring with the scantiest bit of instruction. He'd balanced that job with working on the ranch, training horses and riders. Three little girls had him flummoxed.

She stepped past him. "Delivery!" Her smile didn't need to be forced. "Delivery from Taters and Tales." She held up two bags in her right hand and a smaller one in her left.

"*Komm* in," he urged as he led the way into the house, then raised his voice as the shrill cries from within increased in volume. "I don't know how two little girls can make so much noise."

"Easy. They open their mouths and bellow. Same as cows and goats and sheep." She handed him the three bags.

She didn't pause to admire the great room with its living space, dining area and kitchen. A door led, she knew, to a bedroom where the girls probably slept. Another sleeping space was in the loft. A maple leaf quilt in a variety of brightly colored blocks hung over the railing. She was astonished to see no toys, and the three books she'd given the girls were the only sign *kinder* lived in the house. Two were on the floor. Where was the one she'd given Ella?

Then another shriek rent the air. Taking a deep breath, she strode to the dining table where the three little girls were seated, Ella holding onto her book. There were four plates on the table, but no silverware. She understood why when she saw the two plates in front of Ella and the spot where Daryn had intended to sit were topped by peanut butter sandwiches. Kayla's and Rae-Rae's plates were empty. Crumbs and smashed bread littered the floor under Rae-Rae's high chair. Had Kayla eaten her sandwich?

No, Carrie realized with a smothered chuckle. Kayla's sandwich—or at least part of it—must be what was sitting on Daryn's head.

"Daryn," she said as if nothing was amiss, "put the bags on the table, and once everyone is ready for supper, we'll look and see what's inside them."

The girls stared at her as she put her purse on the table

next to the bags. Kayla's mouth was open in mid-cry, but she closed it when Ella reached over and tapped her arm. Rae-Rae bounced in the high chair in excitement.

"Caw-rie!" she called, waving her hands to be picked up.

"Time for supper." Carrie wanted to scoop up the *boppli*, but she knew suppertime must be peaceful. Without turning, she said, "We'll wait while *Onkel* Daryn washes his hair."

"Hungry now!" insisted Kayla.

"Everyone is, but food should be on the table. Not on our heads."

Kayla pouted while Rae-Rae regarded her with confusion. Ella seemed to understand the jest. She didn't smile, but amusement flickered in her eyes.

Gut! Ella was listening, though she wasn't taking part in the conversation.

Looking at where Daryn was staring at her in amazement, she flicked her fingers at him. "Go and wash your hair. The food will wait." She re-aimed her smile at the table. "So will the girls."

"If you'd rather—"

"*We*," she said, putting enough emphasis on the word that the younger girls began to smile, too, "would rather not eat while you have supper on your skull."

She picked up the plates from the table and followed Daryn, who headed for the kitchen sink. "Do you need help washing out the peanut butter?"

"I can handle it."

"*Gut.*" Lowering her voice as he grabbed a towel from a ring by the sink, she said, "Perry mentioned you asked him to join you at Kolton's farm tomorrow. He's excited to see the bison."

"He'll have to behave himself. It's important to stay calm around those big animals. I figured if anything could impress on him he shouldn't be throwing his weight around, it'll be a bison."

"That'll work out great!"

His eyes narrowed. "What will?"

"You and Perry going to the Lehman farm. I spoke with Ruthie this afternoon. She's willing to watch your girls in the morning, so you can take them with you when you go."

"She's already got two *kinder* to deal with."

"Who are the perfect ages to play with your girls."

"Those *kinder* need her attention. I can't ask her to watch three more—"

He lowered his eyes, and she knew he couldn't make himself describe his nieces as troubled, though they were. She didn't halt herself from putting her hand on his arm in sympathy. His muscles tensed beneath her touch, but eased when she said, "Daryn, she wants to help."

"That's nice of her."

"But?"

"No but," he said, pulling his arm away from her fingers. "I appreciate her offer, and I'll talk to her about it. Having her watch the girls in the morning will help."

"I'll watch them in the afternoons."

His eyes almost popped out of his head. "You? But you've got a job. Two with the food trailer."

"If I've got an event coming up for the trailer, they can help me get the trailer ready."

"Have you had *kinder* help? The job takes a lot longer." A grudging hint of humor filtered in his voice. "I know that for a fact."

"I know how to work with kids, too, and if you keep an eye on Perry when he's not with *Daed* and Gerald, I'll have time for your nieces. See?" She gave him a smile. "Nice and neat."

He stared at her as if trying to determine if she was serious. "I'll rinse my hair and be right back."

She didn't move as he rushed away as if a pack of rabid coyotes nipped at his heels. What was his problem?

Figuring that out was impossible, so Carrie went to the table. She opened her purse and pulled out a brush. The girls' hair looked as messy as it had yesterday.

"While we're waiting for your *onkel*, do you want me to braid your hair?" she asked.

Rae-Rae glanced at Kayla and grinned when her big sister smiled and nodded. Both girls gasped along with Carrie when Ella jumped to her feet. Grabbing her book, she raced into the bedroom and slammed the door behind her.

"What did I say wrong?" Carrie posed the question to herself.

Kayla answered, "Ella no like mirrors."

Dropping to sit in the chair between the two little girls, she whispered, "Why?"

"Mirrors empty. Only Ella. No Eli."

Carrie swallowed her gasp. Since her twin sister had jumped the fence Carrie had tried to explain how she felt to herself and to others. No words she'd devised had expressed the devastating emptiness with as much pain as Kayla's.

"Eli gone," the littlest one said. Tears bubbled into her eyes before falling along her round cheeks.

It took every bit of Carrie's strength not to cry, too, as she hugged each *kind*. She had hope of seeing her twin again. Ella didn't.

The task ahead of Daryn was greater than she'd guessed. He was depending on her to help him ease the anguish in three young hearts. And his own, too? Was helping the grieving family possible when her heart ached as well?

Chapter Four

"Sorry I'm late," Carrie said a week later as she shoved the farmhouse door closed with her hip and glanced around the kitchen. With a sigh, she noticed the sink was piled high with the breakfast dishes.

A sure sign that *Mamm* was suffering another migraine. When the debilitating headaches struck, her *mamm* had no choice but to remain in her darkened bedroom, prone on her bed. Carrie remembered the first time she'd gone in to take *Mamm* a cup of tea. She couldn't have been more than five or six, and *Mamm* had started having the bouts of agony a few months before, so Carrie hadn't seen her in such pain before. When she'd walked into the shadowed room, she stared at the bed where her gray-faced *mamm* looked like a corpse. Bethany, who had gone in first, had screamed and raced from the room. At the sound, *Mamm* had flinched, proving she was alive. Carrie had noticed that before Bethany's elbow hit hers, splashing hot tea in every direction. Neither had been burned badly, but they'd had to tend to each other because *Mamm* couldn't move to put salve on their splattered burns.

In the fifteen years since, Alberta Detweiler had endured one incident after another. Nothing the rest of the family tried to ease her pain had worked, so Carrie picked up the chores her *mamm* left undone when she sought the sanctuary of dark and quiet.

Though she'd asked Perry to do the dishes before he went to work with *Daed* and the sheep. She grimaced. The teen was more truculent and rebellious with each passing day. Confronting him was a waste of time. He'd say he forgot or blame it on someone else.

Did Daryn have any idea how much she envied him having to deal with three cute little girls instead of a teen who wanted to stay up too late and didn't get out of bed in the morning? This morning, pounding on his bedroom door hadn't roused him. She'd had to send Gerald in to rout him from bed. She and Daryn had their obligations, and they'd agreed to share the duties, depending on each other's strengths and skills. She couldn't expect Daryn to hang over Perry's shoulder.

Patience, she told herself. They needed to give the younger ones a chance to see that being part of a family was the best way to heal broken hearts.

Putting the bag with the take-out containers on the table, Carrie paused as she was about to open the refrigerator. What was Daryn's relationship with the rest of his family? As far as she knew, they lived in Canada. The idea of asking him such a personal question was unsettling because he didn't offer much information about his nieces.

Footfalls sounded on the back porch along with running water. *Daed*, Gerald and Perry must be washing up before coming in for their midday meal. That was her signal to have everything ready. If she hadn't been kept late at the diner, she would have made them soup and sandwiches. As it was, they'd have to do with the omelets and pancakes she'd brought from the diner. Ketchup, syrup, butter, pickles, applesauce and chow chow were soon set on the white tablecloth that was embroidered with daffodils and lilacs. She placed cups, plates and silverware in front of the chairs where they each sat. A pinch of dismay taunted her when she left Bethany's spot empty.

Perry had been curious the day after he'd arrived in Lost River why they didn't use her twin's seat. The curt answer he'd gotten from *Daed* must have convinced him not to ask questions.

"*Komm* in!" Carrie said as she motioned to the table before opening the bag. "I've got two bacon omelets and three Spanish ones with jalapeños as well as a double order of scrambled eggs and corned beef and two servings of pancakes with bacon. So help yourself."

"Jerek, you choose first," her *daed* said.

Carrie turned toward the door in surprise. Their bishop, who edged around her brother, was a head shorter than Carrie. A spry man with a huge gray beard that dropped to the front of his white shirt and twinkles in his eyes, he resembled a leprechaun. Unlike an Irish elf, he was long to thought and slow to speech, always considering every word before he spoke it.

Curious what had brought the bishop to their house, Carrie opened the insulated container that held *kaffi*. She filled the cups as the men found seats around the table. *Daed* must have explained to Jerek that *Mamm* was suffering another of her bad headaches because the bishop didn't ask about her. Jerek motioned for Carrie to sit so they could share a silent grace before they ate.

Beside her, Perry's stomach growled, and she heard him mutter something that sounded like, "Now? Now? Now? Starving here." His voice was so low she doubted anyone else heard it, and she tried to focus on her gratitude to God, adding her thanks for Him inspiring her boss's generosity. Lou Spanos had sent the food home with her after asking Carrie to work an extra hour because her boss knew Carrie's family would be eager for the food and that she had limited time before leaving for the Lehman farm to collect Daryn's nieces. Lou had owned the Central Valley Diner for fifty years, and her heart was as big as her gigantic burgers.

Listening to Perry continue to complain under his breath, she thought how she and Bethany used to whisper together during silent grace. They'd been closer in age to Ella than to her cousin, but they'd known they should be quiet and delighted in the mischief. The memory should have been a sweet one, but it was another reminder of how disconnected she was from her twin. The life she'd imagined they'd share was gone.

She gave her cousin's ankle a sharp nudge with the side of her shoe. He flinched, then glared at her. She lowered her eyes as he became silent. Taking her frustration with Bethany's departure out on Perry wasn't fair. She asked God's forgiveness and would do the same with her cousin later.

Jerek said, "It smells *wunderbaar*, Carrie." It was the signal to end their prayers and raise their heads. "Is this Lou's cooking?"

"*Ja.*" She smiled.

"What a treat!"

Daed chuckled. "Let us know when you might be hankering for Lou's food, and Carrie would be happy to bring it home from the diner. Ain't so, Carrie?"

"Anytime." She didn't let her smile fade, though she couldn't help thinking that buying food for everyone would cut into the small amount she hoped to squirrel away for hiring a private detective to find Bethany. On the other hand, Lou would send plenty of food with Carrie if she knew Jerek would be there. The *Englisch* cook and the plain bishop had been friends for longer than Carrie had been alive. From what Lou had said, Carrie guessed Jerek had helped her boss through her grief after her husband was killed in a hunting accident.

Carrie forced her thoughts to the present. "What would you like today, Jerek?"

After the bishop had selected pancakes, *Daed*, her brother and Perry grabbed the two omelets and the scrambled eggs. Carrie picked up the container with the second order of pancakes. She thanked the bishop when he handed her the bottle of maple syrup, which had been sent from Vermont by a friend her parents had made there while working on disaster relief after a hurricane several years ago.

When Perry got the lemonade she'd made yesterday and poured most of it into a glass, Carrie knew she would have to make more that evening after returning from Agua Estrella Ranch. Her cousin downed quarts of it every day, whether at home or the diner. He had a real sweet tooth, and she was surprised he hadn't chosen pancakes. Then she realized that pancakes and lemonade would be horrible together.

"I hear you're watching the Byler girls this afternoon, Carrie," the bishop said before taking a sip of his *kaffi*.

"*Ja*," she replied. Was this the reason why Jerek was there? Curiosity or something more? "Ruthie Lehman can watch them until I can get away from the diner, and then I plan to go over to Agua Estrella Ranch and spend the rest of the day with them until Daryn is finished with work."

"How are they doing?"

This was the real reason he was visiting. Jerek took his duties as their leader seriously, and he was concerned about the community's three newest members.

Carrie set her fork on her plate next to her untouched food. "Confused and grief-stricken. They're so young, and they've lost so much."

Jerek nodded. "That's not surprising. We adults fail to

understand God's plan too often. How can we expect *kinder* to comprehend what He has in store for us?"

She passed the container holding the bacon to the bishop when nobody answered. There wasn't an answer.

As if she'd spoken her thoughts aloud, Jerek went on, "As adults, we can choose when and how to mourn. We choose happiness when we're ready for it. For *kinder*, it isn't as easy. All they understand is the here and the now. Tomorrow is as far away for them as the beginning of the next millennium."

Daed asked, "Are any other members of the Byler family planning to move to Lost River? It might be easier for the girls if they saw someone they knew."

Carrie was startled by the question, wondering why she hadn't asked that herself. "I don't know."

Jerek reached for the milk container and splashed more into his cup. "Daryn hasn't mentioned anything about his family. From what I've heard, he lived in Canada."

"Prince Edward Island, though the girls lived somewhere in Missouri before they came here."

The men's eyes focused on her, and Carrie wished she'd remained silent.

"The little girls have shared bits and pieces. They don't talk about their pasts much." *Especially if Ella is there*, she added in her mind. Anything she'd learned from chatty Kayla and little Rae-Rae had been when their older sister was elsewhere.

And their *onkel*, she realized, as *Daed* began to discuss the weather—an always safe topic in the valley where a storm could sweep down or vanish in seconds. She wished she could switch off her unsettled thoughts, but she couldn't ignore how the littlest girls took care never to mention their family when Daryn was around. Were they keeping secrets from him, or had they discerned with their childish insight how much pain any mention of such things caused him?

He'd failed to see how the *kinder* already depended on him. Not just for food or a roof over their heads. They needed him to prop up their broken hearts, but he didn't seem to recognize that. There must be some way she could help him see the truth. Praying God would guide her to discover it, she began to wash the dishes while she listened to the conversation at the table.

It had turned from the weather and the haying that was being done on most of the valley farms back to Daryn and the girls and their family. She looked around the table, anxious to discover what the bishop might have learned that would give her a way to help Daryn's nieces.

Jerek had finished his pancakes and was refilling his *kaffi* cup.

Slouched in his chair and nursing his glass of lemonade, Perry was trying to make himself seem invisible. His sideways glances at the bishop were as obvious as a shout. He wasn't comfortable in Jerek's company. Did he think the bishop had called in order to chastise him for the fight at the diner?

Sympathy coursed through her. The teen acted like a beaten dog, snarling at everyone who came near. Telling him he was starting with a clean slate in Lost River—or nearly clean—wasn't something he would have believed. She sighed. When a person was told he or she was a certain way, it was too easy to start believing it. How could they convince Perry there was more to him than a miscreant?

"A clean break from what the girls have known may seem difficult," *Daed* said, "but sometimes it can be a blessing."

"Like a bandage pulled off quickly?" Jerek asked.

Gerald wrinkled his nose. "I hate when people say that."

He held up his arm and ran his finger along the hair growing there. "Pulling off the bandage can hurt worse than the original injury."

Carrie collected the empty containers, hoping nobody saw her smile. For such a big man, her brother could act like a petulant toddler. She paused on her way to the trash can when the back door opened. Her eyes widened when Daryn walked in, his shoulders bent. A glance at the clock told her why he was there. She'd told him she'd get to the Lehman farm by one. It was almost two.

Before anyone else could speak, Gerald surged to his feet. He leaned forward with his hands fisted on the table. "What do you want?"

Carrie fired a frown at her brother, but he was impervious to her expression because he'd seen it often.

Jerek patted Gerald's hand. Though the bishop didn't speak, his message was clear. Guests should be welcomed, not reviled.

Perhaps Daryn had noticed the bishop's action, too, because he said, "I'm only here to pick up Carrie to take her to the Lehmans' farm to get the girls. She's watching them this afternoon." He glanced at her. "You aren't, ain't so?"

"I am. I—"

Her brother interrupted her. "Why? Carrie can drive herself. She…" Gerald's voice faded as he glanced at Jerek. He didn't sit, but straightened, relaxing his hands.

Carrie eased past her brother. How could Gerald be so rude when their bishop was sitting at the table? Hoping her face wasn't as bright red as it felt, she said, "Daryn, let me finish clearing the table, and I'll be ready to go."

"I'll wait outside."

"*Ja*," growled Gerald.

At the same time, Carrie asked, "Have you eaten?"

"Sit with us." *Daed*'s voice was cool, but he motioned for Daryn to join them.

Gerald retook his seat, but his glare gauged every step Daryn took toward the table. Greeting their bishop and her *daed*, Malachi, Daryn sat in the empty chair beside Jerek.

Or he started to. He froze when Gerald echoed Carrie's gasp. Halfway between standing and sitting, Daryn asked, "What's wrong?"

"Nothing is wrong," Jerek said. "Sit and make yourself comfortable, Daryn."

Carrie's hands trembled as she got a clean plate. She set them in front of Daryn along with a knife, fork and spoon. Drawn into the conversation *Daed* and Jerek had been having, he answered with respect and as much thoughtful consideration as the bishop. She appraised *Daed*'s reaction and was glad to see he was listening intently to Daryn. Gerald had gone silent. Because Daryn was sitting in their sister's chair or because he was in their house?

As she sorted the carryout containers and put what could be composted into the bin, Carrie was surprised when she heard chairs scraping the floor as the men rose. Daryn was finished already? She rinsed her hands and dried them before grabbing her black bonnet off its peg. Daryn was at the door by the time she reached it.

"Carrie?" called Gerald.

She prayed he wouldn't make another snide comment, but it was for naught.

"When will you be back with *the girls*?" His slight emphasis on the words made it clear he didn't want her bringing Daryn with her.

"We're going over to the ranch. I'll stay with them until Daryn gets home, and then I'll head straight home."

It irritated her that she needed to explain her plans for

the day, but she didn't want her brother showing up at the ranch. He didn't need to worry about Daryn spending much time with her. He was working with Kolton Lehman today. Other than the ride over to the farm, they wouldn't have any time together until Daryn came home tonight after work.

But then Carrie realized they wouldn't even have the ride to the Lehman farm together because *Daed* asked, "Are you ready to leave, too, Perry?"

Her cousin dragged himself to his feet. Without a word to anyone, he grabbed his straw hat and strode out. It was, Carrie knew, going to be an uncomfortable trip to the Lehman farm.

Daryn couldn't remember any time he'd been less comfortable than at the Detweilers' table. If Jerek hadn't been sitting there, he would have left, frustrating Gerald, who wanted an argument. Swallowing his lunch as fast as he could, though it was delicious, had seemed the wisest course.

"Perry, take the farm wagon," he said, pointing to the vehicle he'd borrowed from the ranch. "We'll follow in the buggy. Carrie will need it to take the girls home."

He choked on the last word because he knew his nieces wouldn't describe the cabin as home. Something he didn't want to think about as Perry walked away at a turtle's pace.

"At this rate, we'll be there before he is," Carrie said.

"He's pretending he's in charge of everything." Daryn sighed. "It's a game. Nothing more. Don't buy into it."

"As you didn't buy into Gerald's posturing." She led the way across the wide back porch. "I'm glad you ignored him."

"Okay. Tell me what I did wrong in there."

She flinched. "You didn't do anything wrong."

"So why did you and your big brother give me the stink eye?"

He thought she might not answer him as she stepped off the porch. At an intersection beyond the far corner of the lawn, two cars were waiting at the stop sign for a tractor to rumble past. The spring breeze stirred dust along the side of the road and shook the grass and scrub bushes.

"You chose the seat where my sister used to sit," she said without looking at him.

"You mean you don't use the chair at all?"

"I know it's silly." She faced him, the pain from her aching heart blatant on her face. "It wasn't as if we got together and decided. None of us want to sit there because that would mean admitting we believe Bethany won't *komm* home."

"Who's Bethany?"

She stared at him. "You don't know about Bethany?"

He began to shake his head, then frowned. "Is that your sister who jumped the fence?" From what he'd gathered from bits of conversation, the Detweiler daughter had disappeared one night. Nobody knew where she'd gone, though the assumption was she'd left with an *Englisch* boyfriend.

"*Ja.*"

"Older or younger?"

"Bethany is younger by five minutes." She paused, then said, "You should know I don't say anything about being a twin when I'm with your nieces. It could add to their pain."

He was awed by how she kept everyone else's feelings in mind before she spoke or acted. If he'd done that, he might have been able to choose a different path instead of leaving so many places just as he was beginning to feel comfortable there.

Feel at home.

He wasn't sure if he remembered what that felt like. In the past four years, he hadn't stayed in one place more than a year.

Dogs began to bark to his left. Daryn saw over a hundred

sheep in a field. The dogs had gone on guard as he and Carrie walked closer. That he'd expected. What surprised him was how two odd creatures pressed up against the fence as if trying to break through to chase him away. One was black and the other white with large black spots.

"Are those llamas?" he asked in amazement.

"*Ja.*" Carrie's smile returned. "Meet Jackie and Jill. Jackie's the black one, and Jill's the black-and-white one."

"Jackie?"

"When we discovered she was also a female, her name switched from Jack to Jackie." She chuckled. "Nobody was more shocked than Gerald. After my sister suggested we get them, he'd planned to breed them so he could sell the crias—"

"The what?"

"A cria is a llama *boppli*. It's from a Spanish word meaning to bring up or nurse. They're great guardians. As *gut* as the dogs. They don't bark, but they kick and spit and make a racket, which is enough to run off coyotes. *Komm mol.* They're gentle with us as long as we don't pet them on the head. They don't like that."

He remained where he was as she stroked the llamas' backs. The animals were delighted with her attention, but they kept an eye on him. If he shifted as much as a finger, they stiffened. The hoofs at the end of those long legs could do a lot of damage.

Carrie must have realized she wasn't going to coax him over to the llamas, so she headed to where the black buggy sat in front of a whitewashed stable. He followed, glancing back at the strange animals. What would the girls think of them?

Daryn was still asking himself that question at the Lehman farm. He was relieved to see the farm wagon parked in the barnyard as Carrie hurried to the house.

He didn't follow, walking instead toward the vast pasture where Kolton kept his bison. No matter how many times he viewed them, he was always impressed by their bulk and serenity. The large cows wouldn't hesitate to protect their calves from predators, even from wolves.

Going to the fence, he watched as the mighty beasts grazed. He heard Kolton's and Perry's voices from one of the barns, but he couldn't pull his gaze from the bison. How he'd love to have such a healthy herd! He was soaking up all he could from Kolton, who'd had the herd for only one breeding season. What Kolton didn't know they worked together to learn. Daryn hadn't guessed he'd find any animal more pleasurable to work with than horses, but he was fascinated by bison.

Someday he would like a herd of his own, but he wouldn't have a roof over his head except for the Marquezes' generosity. He had to remain at the ranch for the foreseeable future.

A tiny form pushed between him and the fence. "Me see!" ordered Kayla.

"Softly," he cautioned. "Bison don't like loud sounds, though they make some."

She put her tiny finger to her lips. "Be quiet. Make bison happy. Pretty bison."

"*Ja.* They're pretty. Pretty big. Pretty magnificent, ain't so?" Daryn laced his fingers through the tightly woven wires of the fence that was as tall as he was. No standard fencing for bison because they were more nimble and powerful than cattle. Though a strand of electric fencing ran along the top, separated from the rest of the section by about six inches, its jolt wouldn't halt a bison if one of the cows or calves took it into their head that they were tired of being in that field.

"What's mag—mag—?" Kayla asked, his niece's eyes on him instead of the bison.

"It means," said a lilting voice from behind him before he could answer, "that the bison are *wunderbaar.*"

He turned to discover Carrie coming toward them, holding his youngest niece's hand while Ella walked by her other side. For the first time that day while he'd been with them, none of the girls were frowning. Ella couldn't hide how glad she was to see Carrie. Kayla ran over to her. Carrie took her hand and gave Ella a wink as if they shared a private joke. His oldest niece relaxed from her vigilant pose. Carrie was again making the connection that eluded him.

How do you make it look so easy? he wanted to shout, but swallowed the words. Instead he said, "Girls, get in the buggy so Carrie can take you to the cabin."

The younger two sprinted across the yard while Ella followed more slowly. Beside him, he heard Carrie sigh. In not much more than a whisper, she said, "I wish she'd act like a *kind.* Ruthie says she doesn't join in with the games the other kids play. She sits and watches, separating herself from everyone but never taking her eyes off her sisters."

"In some ways, she feels as undomesticated as the bison calves."

"I see her more as a tiny songbird."

"Why?" The description was one he wouldn't have devised, so how had she?

"Think about it. If you were to capture a wild bird and put it in a cage near a window, it would bash itself against the bars in a desperate and heart-deep need to return to the fresh air and the open skies. It might kill itself in its attempts to break through. If it didn't, it would pine away, its spirit broken."

"That's how you see her?"

"*Ja.*"

He waited for her to say more, but she turned to look

at the grazing bison who were oblivious to them and their problems. It'd be simple to be envious of the great beasts. If they had food and water and each other, they were content. They didn't worry about the past or the future. Loss was gone as swiftly as joy.

"Would you be willing to give up happiness in order never to know pain?" she asked.

"Are you reading my thoughts?"

A faint smile edged along her lips. "No. There are places even angels are afraid of rushing into."

"And my mind is one?"

"Your words, not mine." Before he could react to her pert retort, she hurried on in a more serious tone. "I know I told you I'd watch the girls in the afternoon, but sometimes I've got to stay late at the diner or get delayed over the midday meal because *Mamm* isn't feeling well."

"What's wrong with her?"

She gave him a quick smile. "Nothing that's contagious, so you don't need to worry about the girls. It's a bad headache, and resting seems to make it go away."

"I didn't mean to pry."

"I know you didn't. Everything changes when kids are involved, ain't so?"

As much of a mess as his life had been before the girls entered it, now everything was more convoluted. So different he couldn't recognize his life as *his*. He could hear Carrie say his life wasn't his any longer. It was his and Ella's and Kayla's and Rae-Rae's mixed together.

When he didn't answer, she went on, "In addition, Daryn, I need to work on Greenie Gal to have everything ready for the arts festival in Dashtown in a few weeks."

A flash of something that felt like panic cramped his gut. "I appreciate—"

"I know you do."

He was shocked that she'd interrupted him, then realized she was trying to tell him what he already knew. Before she'd agreed to watch his nieces, her life had been overfull. Add in three little girls as well as her cousin and a sickly *mamm* to two jobs, he wondered when she found time to sleep.

"Would you have any problem if I work on my food trailer while the girls are with me?" she continued when he remained silent. "None of the heating units will be on while they're in the trailer, but I do have preparations that need to get done."

"Do you have room for all of you in there?"

"I'm used to working in cramped quarters. The kitchen and the storeroom at the diner aren't much bigger than the trailer. We'll manage fine." Her expression suggested she sounded more assured than she felt.

"I'm fine with it if you are."

"*Gut.*"

He stepped in her way as she turned toward the buggy. "You will make sure they stay away from the equipment, ain't so?"

"Daryn, you need to trust me." She met his anxious gaze. "You've asked me to watch them, so trust me to make sure they're safe."

"How can I trust you when I don't trust myself?" The words burst from him before he could halt him.

Shock widened her eyes, and she opened her mouth to speak. Closing it, she ran to the buggy and climbed in. It was gone before he could think of a way to retract the words he'd let loose without thinking.

But how could he when the words were true?

Chapter Five

The spring morning dawned with a bright red sun that warned rain could arrive before nightfall. That was *gut*, Daryn told himself, as he tiptoed onto the porch in his stockinged feet, his boots in one hand and a cup of *kaffi* in the other. For the past two weeks, there hadn't been any precipitation in Lost River. Excellent weather for haying, but the potato farmers were already pumping water from their irrigation systems across their fields.

The horse ranch would suffer if they didn't get rain. Water would have to be trucked to pastures. A *gut* rainy night would solve a lot of problems.

Putting the cup on the floor, he chose a bentwood rocker and pulled on his boots before picking up the cup. He listened to the birds that were greeting the morning from the nearby trees. The windbreak protected the big house and the cabin as well as smaller barns from the strong winds that battered the valley. Those winter storms were past for another year. The gusts coming from the San Juan Mountains to the west were warmer. At first, he'd called them chinook winds, but had been told the term was reserved for the gentle winds that swept the eastern flanks of the Rocky Mountains.

Not that it mattered. The breezes marked the end of winter and were laden with precious rain that helped hay, potatoes and other crops grow. However, it was water from the aquifer flowing beneath the whole valley that made farming possible.

Daryn gazed across the yard to the Marquezes' big house where lights were on. His boss, Carlos, and his boss's wife, the vet everybody called *Doktor* Lynny, must be having their morning *kaffi*. Muffled noises came from the bunkhouse, and he knew the men in there were getting ready for the day.

He took a sip and strained his ears for any sound inside the cabin. The girls had been asleep when he checked them before slipping outside. Ella had been lying on her back, her bedding as neat as when she went to bed last night. Kayla's bed, on the other hand, looked as if someone had been wrestling tigers. Every corner had been pulled out, and her pillow was on the floor. Somehow, Rae-Rae had maneuvered herself from the head of the bed to the foot. Her pillow had traveled with her as she lay on her stomach with her bottom in the air and her bare toes tucked under one edge of the blanket.

Did that say something about their personalities? If so, it was a clue he couldn't read. The girls continued to treat him as an unwanted stranger. More than once in recent days, Rae-Rae had started to talk to him, chattering as she did with Carrie. Then she'd become quiet. Why? Had her older sisters told her to give him the silent treatment? Why would they do that?

He clenched the cup handle so hard it creaked. Loosening his grip before he broke it, he sighed. Maybe asking for Carrie's help had suggested to the girls that he didn't want them in his life. He wished he could explain how he felt. He was touched that his sister had arranged for him to watch over her most precious possessions, but he wasn't sure she'd made the right decision.

Perhaps he should ask Carrie's opinion again on steps he could take to get his nieces to feel more comfortable with him. Not that he'd had a chance to talk with her. He saw her when she brought the girls to the cabin each afternoon while he was working with the ranch's horses. When it was time for her to leave before supper, her brother arrived to take her home.

Did Gerald believe she was in peril from a man who might lead her into trouble?

Daryn wanted to snort at his thoughts. Trouble? He knew it well, real trouble and transgressions he'd been wrongly accused of. He glanced to the north and the blue-gray mountains. He'd thought he'd be happy in Wyoming until he made the mistake of letting himself believe Mindi Malone, his boss's daughter.

The lies she'd spun with skill had enticed him, and he'd never imagined she wasn't being honest. That's why he couldn't fault his boss who'd swallowed hook, line and sinker the tale she'd told to convince her *daed* that she'd been innocent. She'd persuaded his boss the accident when she'd stolen a car and crashed it into a length of fence and its consequences of letting a herd of young cattle escape, some of them wandering away and dying, had been Daryn's fault. Daryn had been in trouble with the authorities before, so it was easy to believe this was another example of how he'd messed up wherever he'd gone.

Or had she actually swayed her *daed* to accept her lies? Neil Malone had arranged for Daryn to work at the Agua Estrella Ranch for his *gut* friend. Why would he have done that if he accepted everything his daughter said?

So many questions Daryn couldn't answer. Didn't have

time to answer because he needed to be focused on his nieces' needs. He had asked God's forgiveness for what he'd done, taking full responsibility for his errors, but how could he find peace of mind when he didn't know how to deal with what he *hadn't* done?

He couldn't go to Jerek to share his mistakes. Confessing to things he hadn't done would have been another lie, and accepting help would urge him to lower his guard. He'd done that before when he was a teen in Prince Edward Island, and the people he'd thought were his friends disappeared after painting a neighbor's boat with obnoxious graffiti, leaving him to face the consequences by himself.

Daryn put his unfinished *kaffi* on the porch and stood. A single glance through the front window allowed him to see Rae-Rae was asleep. If the other two were stirring, she would be too. She was a light sleeper and determined to participate in everything her sisters did. He wanted to tell her following others was the best way to find herself mired in disaster.

"Stop it!" he muttered to himself as he walked across the yard that separated the cabin from the nearest paddocks. Looking back at the past would keep him from moving forward with his life. Not just his, but the lives of three little girls, too.

Leaning on the fence, Daryn smiled as he watched a palomino moving through the paddock in the sunshine. A short time ago, the horse's gait had been uneven. It wasn't smooth now, but better. He whistled, and the quarter horse came toward him.

"Pretty!" crowed Kayla.

Daryn almost jumped out of his skin. What was the four-year-old doing outside by herself? Her hair was tangled, and her nightgown dragged in the dust as she inched along the railing toward him.

"*Gute mariye.*" The little girl waved as if she hadn't seen him in days.

He was about to chide her, reminding her how he'd told the girls to stay in the house or on the porch. Then he saw the excitement in Kayla's eyes. He remembered how he'd felt the same exhilaration when he was her age and admired the fluid strength of his *daed*'s horses.

"He's a beauty, ain't so?" he asked her, offering his hand. He was amazed when she took it.

She grasped the fence with her other hand. "Pretty horsey gots name?"

"*Ja.* It's Mantequilla. That means butter in Spanish. He's the color of butter, ain't so?"

"Pretty name." When she tried to repeat it, she couldn't.

Having sympathy, he said, "We call him Monty."

"Monty. Like that." For the first time, she looked at him instead of the horse. With a coy smile, she said, "Like riding, too."

"You ride?" he asked with care. The girls weren't always truthful, telling him only what they thought he should know.

"*Ja...* No." She hung her head. "Needs someone to help."

He almost asked, "Don't we all?" He instead asked her a few more questions. From what he could decipher from her mixed-up answers, she'd ridden a couple of times with someone leading the horse and a second person holding her. That was about what he would have expected from what his sister had written in her letters.

The family had had a vegetable farm with a farmstand by the road, so the horses Kayla had been familiar with would have pulled equipment and the family's buggy. They wouldn't have been the sleek animals the Marquezes kept at the ranch for riding and rehabilitation.

Without hesitation, she stepped forward so he could pick her up. He tried to dampen the triumph bursting through him. Kayla wanted to be close to the horse more than she wanted to avoid him.

"Slowly, Kayla," he said as the horse came closer, eager for the treat Daryn often brought him. "Horses are big. We need to be quiet and not make any sudden moves. Let Monty *komm* to us."

The little girl bit her lower lip and quivered with excitement as the horse edged along the fence.

"How are you doing, Monty?" Daryn asked in a low voice. "How's that leg? It doesn't look as if it's bothering you too much this morning."

"Ride him?" she asked.

"Not now." When she pouted, he hurried to say, "Monty had a boo-boo on his leg, and *Doktor* Lynny wants it to get better before anyone rides him."

"Like my boo-boo?" She held up her chubby arm where the remnants of a scrape were barely visible.

"*Ja.* Like yours. Monty's is getting better, too." No need to share that the horse's injury had been far more serious, so serious *Doktor* Lynny had been unsure if the animal would survive it.

He'd been impressed with the veterinarian's dedication. Monty wasn't a fancy purebred. He'd been an abused animal brought to the ranch because the charity which rescued him thought putting him down was the most humane thing they could do. *Doktor* Lynny had seen determination in Monty's eyes and decided he was a fighter, so she'd battled his wounds and infection. Soon he would return to the life he'd been meant to have.

Daryn envied the horse. Monty's life was going to be great. Though the horse had endured tough times, he was set now.

Was Daryn? He'd been at the ranch for a year. That was the most time he'd stayed in one place since he'd left Prince Edward Island, and he hadn't been on the island long. He'd seen Carlos glancing in his direction when another employee moved on to a different job, especially since Daryn had arranged to work part-time at the Lehman farm to learn more about raising bison.

"Pretty horsey." Kayla's delight pulled him from his dour thoughts.

"*Ja.*"

He set the little girl on her feet. With an excited giggle, she ran to where her sisters were on the porch. Rae-Rae smiled in response to her sister's excited recital of how Kayla got to pet the horse, but Ella frowned. She aimed her scowl at him before leading her chattering sisters into the cabin. It was as if she refused to be happy, not even for her younger sister.

As he stared at the stern set of Ella's shoulders, he realized he and his oldest niece might be more alike than either would admit.

That afternoon as the breeze from the north smelled of falling rain, Daryn heard a buggy slowing to a stop in front of the cabin. Its metal wheels had a unique sound on the gravel along the road. Poking his head out of the stable to confirm it was a plain buggy, he told the farrier working on the last of the horses that he'd be right back.

"Okay," the farrier said as he pried the worn horseshoe off a horse used for beginner riders. The old bay was as patient with having its shoes changed as she was with the youngsters who were learning to ride.

Beside him, Carrie's cousin, Perry, was watching with interest. More interest, in fact, than Daryn had seen him take in any work around the ranch or at the Lehmans'. Maybe the teen wanted to become a blacksmith. It would be a *gut* trade because the few smiths around Lost River had more work than they could handle.

"Perry, will you stay and help Leon?" he asked in what he hoped sounded like a carefree tone.

It didn't matter because the teen leaped at the chance, stepping forward to grab the bucket holding the tools the farrier needed. He snatched it from Daryn's hand so fast the pail banged against Perry's leg. The kid whirled to assist the dark-haired man and began to ask questions. Leon looked over his shoulder and arched his brows.

Daryn shrugged. Who would have guessed the teen had enthusiasm for any aspect of ranch life?

As Daryn emerged from the small stable, Carrie stepped out of the buggy and turned to help his youngest niece. Ella and Kayla jumped down. They were talking, but Ella stopped when she saw him. Wanting to believe it was coincidence, he couldn't when Carrie flashed him a gentle smile of sympathy. Vexation flooded him. He didn't want to be an object of pity.

Kayla rushed to him and flung her arms around his legs. "We sees kitties in the barn. Lots of kitties."

"That's *gut*," he said, focusing on her while Carrie settled Rae-Rae on her hip and walked toward them. He noticed how Ella remained by the buggy, tapping her toe in obvious impatience. He wanted to ask who had taught her such behavior, but didn't. Talking about their past with their parents was a guarantee he'd upset the girls as well as himself. "Cats are *gut* hunters. Ruthie and Kolton won't have to worry about rats getting into their chicken feed."

"Can we have a kitten?" Kayla flung out her hands. "No wants rats here, ain't so?" Her eyes widened. "We gets chickies, too. Chickies and kitties. No rats."

"Let's talk about it later."

"That means no," said Ella, who'd edged closer while his attention had been on her sister. "Doesn't it?"

He stared. How he'd prayed that she'd speak to him, but he hadn't imagined it would be like this. Sharp, frustrated, with contempt. When he started to reply, Carrie shook her head. It wasn't easy to ignore Ella's tone, but it'd be worse if he silenced her again.

"No kitties? No chickies?" asked Rae-Rae before popping her fingers into her mouth.

He answered before the two younger girls burst into tears. "The ranch isn't mine. We'll talk with *Doktor* Lynny. Okay?"

"Soon?" asked Kayla.

"Soon."

"Then get kitties and chickies, *Onkel* Daryn?"

He must have answered, though he had no idea what he'd said. It seemed Carrie had sent the girls inside, because they hurried up the steps and into the cabin.

"Are you okay?" Carrie asked through the roar in his skull.

"I'm not sure."

"If having a kitten is a problem—"

"Did you hear what she called me?" Words began to flow from his mouth, easing the paralysis of shock. "It's the first time one of them has called me *onkel* or used my name. Before, it's been sort of a 'hey, you' situation."

Her smile warmed him more. "That's splendid, Daryn,

but I'm not surprised. Kayla hasn't stopped talking about you and the horse you let her pet. I'm not sure she took a breath all the way from Ruthie's house. Said you picked her up so she could get near the horse."

"She would have let anyone help her get close to Monty."

"Be grateful, Daryn. As Jerek says, a small blessing—"

"Is still a blessing. I get that, but this one step forward, two step back dance is frustrating."

"I know."

He looked at her, *really* looked at her. She appeared cheerful and carefree, but a faint cloud around her revealed she was carrying an invisible burden she didn't want to share. Had it always been there? He'd been so wrapped up in his problems he hadn't paid much attention to hers.

It was time to change that. She was doing so much to help. He needed to return the favor.

"Can you sit for a minute?" he asked, motioning toward the bentwood chairs on the porch. When she hesitated, he added, "The windows are open, so we'll be able to hear the girls."

"They plan to get their coloring books. The ones with cats in them." She chose the rocker, so he sat on the straight back chair beside her. "Ruthie mentioned Kolton's sister's kids had a kitten when they lived here."

"*Danki* for the heads-up. I want to give you a heads-up on Perry."

She stiffened. "Is something wrong?"

"The opposite." He shared what he'd seen in the stable. "You might want to talk to Malachi about having Perry apprenticed to a blacksmith."

"*Daed* will be happy to hear that. Working with a smith should wear Perry out so he won't have the energy to look for trouble."

"Don't take your eye off him completely. Kids his age don't have to look for trouble. It seems as attracted to them as iron is to a magnet."

It was the truth. No matter how hard his family had worked to keep him from finding mischief, he managed to get himself into trouble up to his chin. Had the tales of his ignoble exploits—both real and the ones enhanced by the repetition of gossip—reached her? He hated the idea of her being bombarded with half-truths and outright lies about his misdeeds as well as the truth. She treated him with respect. He was aware how fragile his reputation was and how swiftly it could be destroyed.

Only this time, three little girls depended on him.

Carrie broke the silence. "My brother reminds me of that at least once a day."

"Because of Perry?"

"Because of my twin. He refuses to give me or himself a chance to make the mistakes Bethany did." She rolled her eyes. "Listen to me. Complaining about something that won't be changed when I should be thanking you for taking such interest in my cousin. I'll talk to *Daed* tonight. He'll know if someone is looking for an apprentice." Standing, she said, "*Danki*, Daryn. This may change Perry's life."

He came to his feet, too. "It'll be his choice. All we can do is give him a gentle shove in the right direction."

"He's stubborn. He may need more than a gentle shove."

"From what I saw, he won't need much urging. The boy was thrilled with the chance to help Leon."

"I'm so grateful you noticed his interest in learning more."

As her steady gaze met his less-certain one, thoughts of the teen vanished. Instead, he began to think of what he himself wanted. He couldn't think of anything he wanted more than this beautiful woman in his arms as he sampled her lips that looked deliciously soft.

Don't be a dummkopf! He shifted his eyes away. What if his past caught up with him? If he had any feelings for Carrie—even friendship—he should avoid doing anything that would draw her into the mire his life could become.

In an off-hand tone, he said, "Looks like the rain is going north of us."

There was a beat of silence before she replied. "*Daed* says there will be rain in the valley by week's end, and he's usually right." She motioned for him to let her pass so she could check on the girls. "His accuracy is better than the TV weatherman's, according to patrons at the diner."

"Is that so?" He didn't want to talk about Malachi. He wanted to pull her to him and kiss her. Submerging that thought wasn't easy. In fact, it might have been one of the toughest things he'd ever done.

"*Ja.*" She opened the front door and gasped.

"What's wrong?"

"Was there a tornado in here?"

Daryn grimaced as he followed her in, taking care to step over blocks and a stuffed cat. He'd meant to pick up the house earlier, but Leon had arrived ahead of time. So instead of cleaning up after his nieces, he'd gone to the stables. He bent for a small sneaker, then left it. Carrying a single shoe into the bedroom would be like taking a lone grain of sand off a beach.

The girls were on their bellies, intent on their coloring, or pretending to be. He decided it was the latter when Rae-Rae glanced toward them, then at her coloring book as her older sisters hissed warnings.

Carrie must have heard, too, because she told the girls to

put down their crayons and pick up their clothes and toys. As she pitched in to help, they obeyed with far less resentment than they would have shown him.

As the *kinder* carried their stuff into their room, Carrie said, "You can't let them get away with this."

"I know I shouldn't, but if I scold them, they'll never let me into their lives."

"*Kinder* look to adults to give them limits and help them to know right from wrong. We must train them up the way they should go."

He shook his head. "On this you're wrong, Carrie. They barely tolerate me as it is. If I scold them, that would be the end of any chance to make us into a family."

"You've got it backward." When he opened his mouth to retort, she held up a single finger. "Listen to me. I guess you haven't noticed, but I've told them several times what they must do. They might not like it, but they haven't changed their minds about me because I remind them of what's right and what's not."

"But they like you."

"They do like me. In part, because I'm what they expect me to be. Friendly and enthusiastic when they behave and correcting them when they don't."

"If it were that easy for me."

"I know." She put a comforting hand on his sleeve, and a buzz erupted along his whole arm and gathered in his skull, threatening to send his brain reeling. He had to struggle to comprehend what she added. "But part of that is because they don't know what their relationship should be with you. You're not their *daed*, but you also aren't simply an *onkel*. They don't know what you are."

"That's not a surprise. Neither do I."

* * *

Carrie was relieved when Daryn averted his eyes and stepped away from her. He must not have seen the shock that swept across her face when she'd touched Daryn to offer him solace. She hadn't expected such a commonplace contact would create sensations that were anything but common. On the porch, she sensed a new connection between them, but she'd resisted discovering what it was. The moment her fingers settled on his muscular arm, she'd been unable to keep convincing herself it was nothing.

Trying to control her emotions that refused to heed her *gut* sense, she walked over to the table. She bent to pick up a ball that had rolled under it, but halted when she saw a pile of mail on the table. None of the envelopes had been opened, and all had been addressed by the same hand and postmarked in Aylmer, Ontario. There must have been a dozen in the stack.

"Those are from my *mamm*," he said.

"You haven't opened them."

"I will when I have a second to myself." He took the envelopes and tossed them on the coffee table. "Don't lecture me about how I need to answer them. I tell myself that every night, but by the time I can begin to write to her, I'm so exhausted I can't string two words together."

"Why don't you have the girls write to her?"

He frowned as if she'd misplaced her mind. "The girls? Ella might know some letters, but the other two aren't much more than *bopplin*. How do you expect them to write to their *grossmammi*?"

"I don't."

"Then why—"

Not caring she was being rude, she cut him off with, "I don't mean a letter like you or I would write. I meant give them a piece of paper and crayons and let them share something with their *grossmammi* about what's going on in their lives. Does your *mamm* hang pictures made by her *kinskinder* on her fridge with magnets?"

"I guess so."

"You guess so or you *know* so?"

"Why can't you let me give an answer without trying to pick it apart to find some hidden meaning?" He sat on the sofa and stared at the unopened mail. "I haven't been to Ontario for five years, so I don't know if she hangs kids' drawings on the refrigerator like she did when we were kids."

"That's a long time not to see your family."

He started to reply, then paused. Had he been about to say something that would tear away a layer on the barrier he kept between himself and the world? She couldn't imagine what he was trying to hide. Something that made him vulnerable? Or something that revealed anger or another stronger emotion?

"I've got family here now."

Anything she said might deepen the divide between him and his family. "*Ja*, you do. A sweet family. It must feel *gut* to have family. I know I'd miss mine if I didn't see them every day." She chose her words with care, not wanting the conversation to turn to her twin.

"Even Gerald?"

The sparks in Daryn's eyes delighted her. They weren't a smile, but it was a hint that he hadn't always been so somber. She tried to imagine his lips tilted in a grin, the tanned skin around his blue eyes crinkling, as a laugh exploded from him. The first two she could see in her mind's eye, but no sound emerged.

"That's a question I don't think I'll answer."

"Smart of you." He picked up the topmost letter. "Do

you think Ella would cooperate if I asked her to send something to *Mamm*?"

"I don't know, though I'm sure the younger ones will be excited about it. In time, she may become excited, too." She shrugged. "But how are you going to know if you don't try?"

"I don't know." He arched a single eyebrow. "That's the answer you want, ain't so?"

"I want the answer you feel is the truth."

"The truth is I don't have the slightest idea how to reach Ella. She hardly admits I'm alive."

"You're wrong. She is aware of you whenever you're around."

"So she can avoid me."

"That's true, but it's not like she's ignoring you. I'll get the girls started. If you want, you can write to your *mamm* while they're creating pictures for her."

"Yes, ma'am, Teacher Carrie."

She forced her shoulders to ease from their stiff stance and smiled, but she was certain a joint project was the way for his family to reconnect. Would it work? She prayed it would because she was running out of ideas for getting the *kinder* to feel at home with their *onkel* in Lost River. As she was drawn into their lives, it was becoming more difficult to ignore whatever it was that had swept over her when she touched Daryn.

Though she must.

Chapter Six

The Byler girls barely could contain themselves as Carrie drove them to her family's farm the following Monday afternoon. She wanted to help *Mamm* with housework before giving Greenie Gal a cleaning after a successful event in Alamosa on Saturday, and the girls wanted to visit the sheep. The food trucks had offered a variety of food to those who came to watch or participate in a half marathon. She'd given the trailer a lick-and-a-promise cleaning Saturday evening, but hadn't touched it yesterday during the Sabbath. She needed to scrub every surface and decide what she needed to order before the trailer's next excursion.

Parking the buggy by the side of the house, Carrie glanced toward the fields. *Daed* and Gerald had said they were moving the flock this morning. It hadn't gone smoothly, she guessed, because Gerald hadn't shown up at the diner to check on her. She shaded her eyes as she squinted into the sunshine.

There the sheep were! In the field where *Daed* had once grown quinoa.

The crop had been a success until a few years before when yields dropped. Not just on the Detweiler farm, but throughout the valley. The culprit was a fly drilling into the stems to lay its eggs. Work began to find a way to protect the crop, but it had been too late. They couldn't harvest enough to pay their bills. At that point, *Daed* had decided to make a sideline, raising sheep, into their primary business along with selling their hay. It had been enough to get them through the toughest times, and the sheep were becoming a well-established flock whose lambs were sold for the table or for breeding stock.

It would be a long walk for short legs, so Carrie picked up Rae-Rae before they'd gone far. The other girls managed the quarter mile to the field where the sheep grazed under the watchful eyes of llamas and dogs. Overhead, birds stitched an invisible seam between the clouds floating like whipped cream in the inverted bowl of the blue sky. More menacing clouds were gathering over the mountaintops to the west, but rain, if it came, wouldn't arrive until near sundown because the air was soft and still.

Kayla battered her with questions until they reached the fence and the youngsters saw the llamas, which edged between the flock and the newcomers they didn't recognize. Carrie explained what the llamas did and their names. She doubted the children heard a single word. The llamas and the girls were curious about each other. Did Jackie and Jill move closer because they sensed the *kinder* wouldn't endanger the sheep, or were they intrigued by the smallest humans they'd ever seen?

"Big," Ella said in awe.

"Skinny legs." Kayla shook her head. "I likes horseys more."

Rae-Rae giggled when the llama lowered its head toward her. "Like horseys and l—l—"

"Llamas." Carrie guided her small hand to stroke the llama.

With more giggles, Rae-Rae patted the llama. "Soft. Like blanket."

Carrie didn't have a chance to reply before she heard, "People used to make blankets from their fleeces."

She looked over her shoulder to discover Daryn walking toward them. She shot a scowl at the dogs who hadn't alerted her. When he bent to pet Mutt and Jet, she realized the dogs had accepted him as they did the scholars at the school next door each fall.

Beside her, Ella stiffened, but the other two girls were too focused on the llamas and the dogs to notice their *onkel.*

Putting Rae-Rae on the ground beside her sisters, Carrie went to where Daryn had stopped a few feet away. The sunlight accented a worn spot on the brim of his Stetson.

"What are you doing here?" she asked. "Ruthie told me you were going into town."

"I did, but the supplies Carlos was expecting hadn't arrived yet. When I called back to the ranch, *Doktor* Lynny told me you were going to give the girls a tour of your food trailer. I was hoping I could get in on it."

"Not a tour. We're going to be working on it the rest of the afternoon."

"Could you use an extra set of hands after I take the wagon to Carlos and let him know he'll need to send someone back to town to pick up the shipment tomorrow?"

How could she say no? Not that she wanted to, but a single glance toward the girls told her that Ella wasn't happy about Daryn joining them. Carrie sighed. So far, her attempts to build a bridge between the two had failed.

God, show me the way to bring them together. It was a prayer she'd already made a bunch of times, but she'd keep it going up.

* * *

A half hour later when Daryn still hadn't returned from updating his boss on the missing supplies, Carrie pressed her hands to her lower back as she got to her feet. She'd discovered a bottle of ketchup had tipped over and opened on the bottommost shelf under the trailer's window. The ketchup had spread to the farthest corner. By lying on the floor and stretching so far she was halfway under the other shelf, she dug coagulated tomato sauce from the corner. Her trailer had to be pristine before she opened.

She looked at the three books that would be sitting at one side of her serving window. She always left them in plain sight. *Little Women. Lassie Come Home. Little House on the Prairie.* The first two were wordless requests to her sister. The last was Bethany's favorite book. She knew it was unlikely her sister would see the display but maybe someone else would understand the message and pass it on to Bethany. After all, *Little Women* was about sisters, and Carrie wanted hers to come home, as Lassie had in the book, to their home on the Colorado prairie high in the mountain valley.

It was the clearest request she could have created without putting up a board with the words from her heart. Words that would beg Bethany to contact her.

But what if nobody got the message? If Bethany was in the San Luis Valley, someone would have seen her and word would have reached the Detweilers. Carrie negated that thought. While the area around Lost River was filled with farms, whole swaths of the valley were sparsely populated. Other parts had been claimed by people who didn't want anyone to know their business and they didn't want to get involved with the rest of the world. If her sister had moved into one of those areas, she might as well have hidden herself in one of the craters on the moon. Carrie prayed God would watch over her sister and keep her safe. She'd stopped asking Him to bring her sister home, but He knew what was in her heart.

And Bethany's.

Carrie stared at the space where she'd planned to put an oven for Bethany to make her luscious cakes and breads. It wasn't easy to accept that God had known Bethany's destiny before her sister made her decision to leave, but there was comfort in knowing He was with her twin, no matter where she was.

Stepping over the younger two girls who were napping, curled up like a pair of kittens, she checked on Ella, who was exploring the trailer. The curious *kinder* had touched everything and poked their cute noses into every cupboard. She'd saved Kayla from a cascade of napkin packs, and she'd pulled Rae-Rae aside when a trio of metal mixing bowls tumbled near her. Ella had been far more interested in the griddle and deep fryer, peppering Carrie with questions about how they worked. Not that Carrie could fault the girls. When she'd first looked at the trailer, she'd been as eager as they were to explore every inch of it.

Carrie bent to check the other shelves and found another shelf dotted with specks of mustard and recalled how her friend Paige had said something about having to avoid a careless driver while driving the trailer to the farm. Her fellow waitress at the diner used her pickup to tow the trailer and would have been horrified to discover the mess.

"What's this?" Ella asked as she tried to balance a large wire-metal basket by its long handle.

Carrie hid her surprise as she tried to do each time the five-year-old spoke to her without prompting. "That's a strainer for French fries. It goes into the hot oil and keeps the fries from floating away while they cook."

"Oh." She ran her finger along the handle. "It's big."

"Lots of people like lots of fries. Like you do." She took the basket and tapped the little girl on the nose with her finger, eliciting a rare smile. "It's okay to touch it today, but ask before you do again. It can get hot, and you don't want to get burned."

"Ouch!" she said, widening her eyes that were as blue as the afternoon sky.

"Ouch is right." Carrie set the basket on a nearby counter. "Kitchens can be dangerous. That's why we have to be super-careful when we're in one."

Ella asked, "You're a twin, too, ain't so?"

"I am. How did you know?"

"I heard what you said the other day when you were talking on the porch."

Carrie remembered the conversation. Her twin had been mentioned in passing, but little ears must have been listening closely. Had she and Daryn said anything else they shouldn't have? She couldn't recall, but she needed to let Daryn know to be more cautious.

"Where's your twin?" Ella asked.

She didn't try to squelch her pain as she squatted in front of the little girl. "She left two years ago, and I haven't heard from her since."

"Eli's gone, too."

"I know, *liebling*. It hurts, ain't so?"

Big tears filled the little girl's eyes. "Eli was always there. Now he isn't."

"I understand. I miss talking with Bethany."

"Bethany was your twin?"

Carrie almost corrected her, then halted herself. To say

"Bethany *is* my twin" would be cruel when Ella's twin was dead. Instead she nodded.

Ella patted her hand, then flung her arms around Carrie's neck. Carrie's arms encircled the little girl, drawing her closer. Neither spoke. Trite words of solace would be a waste. Then Carrie realized the little girl wasn't crying as she'd expected. Instead Ella was clinging to her as if she were the only safe place in the world. Carrie could empathize because she was seeking such a haven herself.

Peeling the little girl's arms away, Carrie stood. Going to a nearby drawer, she opened it. "I want you to take care of something for me."

"What?"

Pretending she hadn't heard suspicion in Ella's voice, Carrie pulled out the well-loved stuffed blue calico dog that she'd had for as long as she could remember. Longer, because it'd been a gift from *Mamm's mamm* the day she and Bethany had been born. Carrie had been given the dog, and Bethany's gift had been a stuffed bear she called Patches. The toy had vanished along with her sister, proof to Carrie how precious Patches remained to her twin. Or had Bethany taken it so she could give it to her rumored unborn *boppli* at its birth? So many unanswered questions.

Carrie had set the battered toy on the counter next to the books the first time she opened the trailer for business. She'd become upset when she'd looked over and it'd been gone. A customer had found it on the ground and returned it to her. Unwilling to chance losing it again, she'd left it in the drawer.

She offered it to Ella. "Her name is Freckles."

"Why?"

"Because of the freckles that used be next to her whiskers." Carrie laughed softly, not wanting to wake the others. "Her whiskers are gone, too."

"Along with one ear."

She flipped the shortened piece of black velvet that once had been as long as the floppy one on the other side. "I don't remember what happened to it. Sometimes my brother used to tease me by taking our toys and playing with one of the dogs."

"Poor Freckles." She pointed to a faint scar on her right index finger. "Dogs play hard. I got bit when I played with our dog."

"Ouch!"

The little girl nodded. "Ouch-ouch, but Tilly was a *boppli*. She thought my finger was her toy. That's what *Mamm* said." She lowered her head to hide her face.

But Carrie could sense Ella's grief as if it were a visible halo. "Freckles doesn't bite. She doesn't have any teeth, but she has her tail." She wiggled the piece of woven string that was shorter than it'd been years ago. "It still wags."

Ella made a most unexpected sound. She giggled. It wasn't like the carefree laughs her sisters let loose, but there were wisps of joy in it. Knowing the chuckle was being sifted through her sorrow, Carrie didn't give in to her desire to grab the little girl and give her the biggest possible hug.

She didn't want to send the *kind* scurrying away. Ella, like her sisters, needed to believe she was loved. Grief had stolen her security from her, and it wouldn't be quick or simple to help her trust her heart.

When Carrie arrived with his nieces at the cabin the following day after picking them up from their morning at the Lehmans' farm, Daryn saw her astonishment that he was inside instead of working with the horses. She carried a bag filled with take-out boxes, and he guessed she'd been kept late at the diner. She wore her work apron that was spotted with bits of mustard and drops of *kaffi*.

"I didn't bring enough for you," she blurted.

"No worries. I've already eaten."

"Let me feed the girls before we talk."

He wasn't sure whether to be grateful or annoyed at how she read his mood. Then he realized it must be obvious. He'd been pacing from the sofa to the kitchen counter for the last half hour, too upset to sit.

With an efficiency he had to admire, she got the girls washed and seated at the table. They shared a quick silent grace, and she served sandwiches, chips and glasses of *millich* filled partway. Often the *kinder* spilled as much as they drank.

"Let's talk on the porch," he said when she was finished.

She shook her head. "Let's talk by the stable."

"The girls—"

"They'll be fine." Raising her voice, she called in a cheerful tone, "We're going over to see how Perry is doing in the stable."

Kayla jumped to her feet. "See Monty?"

"Eat first." Carrie's smile suggested everything was as it should be. "When you're done, *komm* to the stable. Wait by the door, and your *onkel* will take you to see the horses. But you've got to eat every bite first. Horses like girls with happy tummies."

Daryn watched in amazement as the girls nodded. As he had so many times before, he wanted to ask her how she handled them with such ease. If he'd made the same suggestion, there would have been pushback and tears from the younger two. Ella would have given him one of her scowls that sent guilt smashing into him.

Grabbing a handful of papers from the table in front of the couch, he followed Carrie to the front door. He started to speak as they walked onto the porch, but she put her finger to her lips and shook her head. Baffled, he matched her steps as they moved away from the cabin.

"It's okay," she said in the same calm tone. "They're so eager to see the horses they won't linger inside and look for mischief."

"Bribery?"

"I'd rather think of it as motivation." For once, she didn't smile.

"Is that why you wanted to speak here?" He stopped by the side of the stable. It was pretty much abandoned on the sunny day. The horses were in the paddocks. Somewhere on the ranch, Perry was repairing fences with two ranch hands Daryn trusted to make sure the teen put in a *gut* day's work.

"No." She faced him. "I didn't want to talk on the porch, because the girls will be eavesdropping."

"Are you sure? Most of what I say they find boring. Or that's how they act."

"Absolutely sure." She outlined what had happened inside Greenie Gal yesterday when Ella had asked about Carrie's twin sister.

The all-too-familiar feeling of a fist sinking into his gut was no longer a surprise. Nor was the corrosive envy that ate at him as he listened to her explain how Ella had opened up to her.

"I wondered where she'd gotten that stuffed dog," was all he said when she finished. Ella spoke to him when necessary. Maybe ten or fifteen words each day, no more, and she would have spoken fewer if she could have.

Her expression showed that she had expected something

else in response. Did she think he was heartless? He had no idea how to help a *kind* who wanted nothing to do with him.

Instead of explaining that, he thrust into her hands the pages he'd brought with him.

"What are these?" she asked.

"You had the girls make pictures to send to their *gross-mammi*. Here are the ones they drew yesterday after supper."

She looked at him as if waiting for him to say more. When he didn't, she glanced at each picture in turn. There were a half dozen, because while Ella had drawn one, Kayla had sketched three scenes. Rae-Rae's scribbles covered two more pages.

Carrie smiled. "Your *mamm* is going to be so happy to have these. I didn't realize Kayla knew some letters. I think that's a *K* there."

He didn't look at the page she held up. "Don't you notice one common thing about the pictures?"

"Are there horses in all of them?"

"No, only in Kayla's. Rae-Rae's are stick figures and squiggles."

"Ella's is a copy of the cover of the book I gave her the day I first met the girls, ain't so?"

"*Ja.*"

"She did a nice job." Raising her head, she said, "I don't see how the pictures have anything in common, other than the *kinder* must have enjoyed drawing them."

"It's more than that." He jabbed a finger at each picture in succession. "They each have you in them."

She looked at the pictures, then shook her head. "How can you tell who Rae-Rae was drawing? They're stick figures."

"Three smaller stick figures. Two larger ones. A man and a woman. I'm assuming—I guess I should say I'm *hoping*

I'm the man because I'm a part of her life, so the woman must be you."

"It could depict Ruthie. They're with her five hours every day."

"But Ruthie has black hair, and you've got blond. Both of the taller stick figures have yellow hair. You and me."

She didn't want to accept what he was saying. Determination tightened her lips as she paged through the drawings again. Holding up Ella's, she argued, "See this? She's drawn Cinderella. Like on her book."

"Take a close look at the princess on the book cover. She resembles you."

"*Ja*, she has blond hair, but I don't remember the last time I wore a hat that looks like an upside-down ice-cream cone. I prefer sneakers to glass high heels."

"But she's tall like you."

She pressed the pages into his hands. "I'm not going to debate this, Daryn. *Kinder* draw what they see around them. I'm around them a lot. So are the horses and so are you and so is Ella's book. Don't read more into it. I'm not trying to usurp your place in their lives."

"Usurp my place?" Had his words suggested that? That hadn't been his intention.

So what had been your intention?

Not an easy question to answer. He couldn't lie to himself. He *had* been hurt when he saw the resemblance to her in the pictures.

"No," he hurried to add, "I never thought that. I wanted you to see how important you are to the girls. I put you in a corner when I asked you to watch them, but they hadn't connected with anyone in Lost River until they met you. I didn't stop to think of what would happen if you couldn't continue to take care of them."

"You're worrying about something that hasn't happened."

"I know, but—"

"Take each day as it comes, Daryn. Enjoy its challenges and its blessings."

"Easy to say."

She smiled. "I know. I didn't tell you everything that happened yesterday."

"What else?" He braced himself, praying for the strength to accept what she had to tell him.

"Ella laughed, Daryn. Not a big laugh, but bigger than a snicker. A giggle."

He grasped her shoulders. "I don't need a whole list of synonyms to describe it. That she laughed is *wunderbaar*."

"It is. I'm sorry it took so long to tell you."

"*Danki* for letting me know." His fingers trailed across her shoulders, and her lips parted with a soft breath he heard more with his heart than his ears. Easing her a half step closer, he was delighted she didn't resist. "Carrie." He had had more to say, but the words vanished as he fell into her green eyes, which were as warm and welcoming as the spring sunshine.

Would she yank herself away if he pressed his lips to hers? Or would she kiss him? They hadn't had any time together as a couple should because they were always surrounded by others. Was that God's way of telling him he should feel gratitude toward Carrie and nothing more?

His questions went unanswered as his nieces rushed toward them, calling his name and hers. A strange expression flashed across her face before she stepped away to greet the youngsters. Relief? Dismay? Uncertainty? He felt those and more as he was pelted with questions about the horses they'd see.

But he didn't have a chance to answer. A tall man strode

toward them, anger billowing off him with every step. What was Gerald Detweiler doing on the ranch in the middle of the day?

Daryn stepped between Carrie's brother and the girls. "Gerald! What can I do for you?"

Carrie's smile became as brittle as antique glass. "I told you I'd meet you at home later."

"I wanted to make sure you were okay," her brother answered.

"And not getting in trouble?" A hint of acidity was a dark undercurrent in her question.

Her brother didn't reply, and Carrie held her hands out to the girls. They stared at Carrie's brother, unsettled by his size and his deep voice.

"You know Gerald," she said to the little girls. "He's my brother, and he worries about me."

When she bent and whispered something to them, Kayla laughed. Daryn felt his shoulders ease from their taut stance.

He had to stop letting Carrie's brother—and other people— make him feel as if he'd instigated some heinous crime and was about to be caught red-handed. He didn't have anything to feel guilty about in the San Luis Valley. Nothing except wishing at the day's end that he'd done better by his nieces. Sitting alone in the living room at night, he would often let the time he'd spent with the *kinder* run through his mind like a never-ending film strip, reminding him of the mistakes he'd made and the opportunities he'd let pass by.

Before walking away, Gerald muttered a warning to his sister that she'd better be home on time.

"You've got to forgive Gerald," she said as they walked with the girls to a nearby paddock where Kayla's favorite horse was grazing.

While the *kinder* chattered about the horse, he said, "For

believing I have wicked intentions if I can get you alone for five minutes." He gave her a wink.

She laughed. "It's a *gut* thing you don't have a mustache. You'd be twirling it like an old-timey villain."

"There wouldn't be any need if your brother stopped worrying about you."

"He's not going to change. He blames himself for letting Bethany go."

"I thought she left in the middle of the night."

"She did. Without telling anyone."

"Does Gerald think that if he'd stood guard day and night it would have made any difference? If your sister was determined to go, she would have found a way."

Resting her folded arms on the fence, she said, "It's his way of dealing with guilt."

He flinched. Though he almost demanded what her brother could possibly know of real guilt—guilt like Daryn carried in his heart—he knew he would have been opening himself to the questions he wanted to avoid. That he must never do.

Chapter Seven

Daryn wasn't sure if Perry had gotten up on the wrong side of the bed or had decided to make everyone around him miserable. Ella had been cooperative this morning in comparison.

It wasn't as if Daryn had asked the teen to do something extraordinary. All the hands on the ranch took turns mucking out the stables and hosing the concrete floors. Perry had completed the job without complaining before, but today, when Daryn came to see how the teen was faring, nothing had been done.

Perry straightened, pushing his black glasses up his nose, when Daryn walked in. Because Perry's hand was stuck in his pocket, Daryn suspected he was hiding a cell phone. That wasn't Daryn's problem unless it continued to keep Perry from doing his work.

Without raising his voice, Daryn said, "I told you to clean the stable."

"I will."

"When?"

"Soon."

Daryn tried to ignore the teen's insolent answer. The words might be different but the tone echoed conversations he'd had with *Daed* in the months before leaving for Prince

Edward Island. As well as ones with his brother later. That had ended with him heading west and leaving his family and—he'd believed at the time—his problems behind him. What a joke!

Did Perry have the same mistaken conviction he was starting from square one and could get away with whatever he wanted? Daryn guessed the answer was *ja*. Arguing wouldn't get through to the kid. It hadn't with him, so he needed to try a new tactic.

Resting his elbow on a stall door, he said, "It's funny, Perry. You think you're making a fresh start. Then you find your problems not only knew where you were headed, but got there before you. They're waiting for you, refusing to let you escape them."

"I don't need you lecturing me. You're not my *daed*. You're not my *onkel*. You're the guy who figured he could get the girl he wants to walk out with to babysit his kids if he tried to get her cousin to walk the straight and narrow."

"Even if that's true, it doesn't change the fact I'm your boss."

"I could quit."

"You could, and then what will you do when you don't have any money? Cell phones aren't cheap."

The teen's face flushed red, then paled. Daryn doubted the Detweilers knew about Perry's cell phone, and the teen liked it that way.

That was confirmed when Perry asked, in a far less aggressive tone, "Will you tell them?"

"It's not my place to confess someone else's transgressions."

"How about your own?" A sly smile edged along the boy's lips. "I heard about how you stole a car up in Wyoming and did a load of damage. Took down a fence. Heard you rustled some of the cows that got out."

Daryn pushed away from the stall door, wondering how that false version of the incident had reached Lost River. "Don't believe everything you hear." Who, he wondered, had learned about that incident and had spread the tale through the ranch? "Clean up in here. Now!"

Striding out, Daryn doubted the teen had any idea the person Daryn was most annoyed with was himself. The consequences of his bad decisions were following him. He had no idea how to make them stop.

When Carrie got to the Lehman farm the next day, the first thing she wanted to do was apologize for being late. Again. There had been a huge rush at the diner before lunch when the highway was closed because of an accident. It hadn't been much more than a fender bender, but the police had shut the westbound lane, so big rig after big rig had pulled into the diner's crowded parking lot. The drivers decided to eat while they couldn't drive any farther.

Each driver, whether man or woman, wanted a large serving with at least one item special ordered. While Carrie and the other waitress, Paige, rushed from table to table to take orders, Lou cooked. They'd spent two hours playing catch-up, and the last meals were being finished and paid for by the time a cop stuck his head past the door to let everyone know the road would be reopening in a few minutes. The diner emptied as if someone had pulled a plug and sent its contents swirling down an invisible drain.

Generous tips had brought smiles from the whole staff, but Carrie couldn't stop thinking of how *gut* it would feel to sit for a half hour or so before she collected Daryn's nieces. Pushing aside her longing to put up her tired feet, she'd hurried at the best possible speed to get the Byler girls. She knew how Ruthie valued punctuality.

Ruthie opened the door as Carrie was stepping onto the back porch. Holding a finger to her lips, her friend said, "Everyone's napping."

Carrie tiptoed into the pleasant kitchen. Despite two young *kinder* and a husband who worked around animals, Ruthie kept every surface shining. It surprised Carrie how much her friend loved keeping house. Ruthie had complained for years about having to pick up after her sloppy brothers. Was it as simple as Ruthie was happy and in love with her husband and her *kinder*? Could love change someone's life that much?

What a stupid question! Love had altered Carrie's life, and she hadn't been the one to fall in love. She was certain Bethany's heart had led her sister away, and it had complicated Carrie's life in ways she couldn't have imagined.

A deep rumble came into the kitchen. She looked into the living room at the front of the house. An elderly man had his head against the sofa, and he was snoring with abandon. Across his lap, Kayla and Ruthie's daughter, Tianna, were draped, matching him snore for snore. Rae-Rae was on a blanket on the floor while Ella was draped over one chair and Ruthie's son, Benny, curled up in another.

"I told you *everyone* was napping." Ruthie walked over to where her ironing board was set near the stove. "*Grossdawdi* Christy and the kids conked out about ten minutes ago."

"I'm sorry I'm late. It was a zoo at the diner."

Ruthie waved aside her words. "You look exhausted. Pour yourself something to drink, and we'll chat until naptime is over."

Grateful to her friend for understanding, Carrie got a glass and filled it with iced tea. She sat at the kitchen table and smiled at her much shorter friend. She noted a slight rounding on Ruthie's belly, a sign her friend was pregnant. Though she wanted to ask when the *boppli* was due, Carrie bit back her questions. Ruthie would tell her when she and her husband were ready to share the glad tidings.

"I'm grateful to *Grossdawdi* Christy," her friend said as she turned the shirt on the ironing board to focus on another section. "He likes to spend time with the *kinder*, and that gives me time to do jobs I don't like as much." Her nose wrinkled. "Like ironing."

Carrie chuckled. "You always avoid pressing seams when we're working at the quilt circle."

"I'd rather wrestle one of Kolton's bison than press seams."

The mention of her husband and his herd gave Carrie the opening she'd been looking for the past week when collecting Daryn's nieces from the farm. "The idea of raising bison seems to be spreading."

"*Ja.* Several farmers have contacted us to buy calves. Kolton plans to keep this lot, but he shares the names of the farms where he bought his cows." She moved the shirt around the ironing board. "Though I wouldn't be surprised if he's willing to part with a few if Daryn wants them. He appreciates how enthusiastic Daryn is."

Carrie hid her surprise. If someone had asked her, she would have said she didn't think Daryn got passionate about anything. He seemed resolved to keep his life on an even keel.

But she couldn't forget how he'd curved his broad hands around her shoulders and gazed into her eyes when she'd told him about Ella's laughter. Hints of the powerful emotions he'd kept hidden had fascinated her then…and every waking moment since. Her dreams hadn't been safe from the memory of how his face had softened a smidgen as his eyes moved from hers to her lips. They tingled at the thought of what might have been if the girls hadn't intruded.

"How well do you know Daryn?" she asked before she could halt herself.

If Ruthie thought the question was odd, no sign was in her reply. "I don't know him as well as Kolton does. Daryn keeps to himself when I'm around. However, Kolton says he can be a real talker when they're discussing the bison." Her eyes narrowed. "You spend as much time with him as my husband does. You must know him as well as anyone around here."

"Like you said, he keeps a lot to himself. I'm curious why he moved here. It's not like he has family here." Her eyes shifted to the sleeping *kinder*. "Or he didn't before."

"You're asking the wrong person. Maybe Kolton knows more."

A deep laugh resonated through the kitchen, and Carrie turned to see Kolton walking in as if on cue. When Ruthie scowled and put her finger to her lips as she motioned with her head toward the living room, the blond man nodded with a smile. He towered over his petite wife, but it was easy to see that she had him wrapped around her smallest finger. A place he was willing to be.

Carrie kept her sigh to herself. She shouldn't have been imagining how it would feel to have a guy look at her as Kolton did Ruthie. She didn't have any place in her life for any complications, and relationships were always complicated.

"What might I know?" he asked as he opened the refrigerator and pulled out the iced-tea pitcher.

"Why Daryn moved to the San Luis Valley when he didn't know a soul here."

Kolton shrugged. "He's never said. Carlos Marquez might be able to tell you. He's the one who offered Daryn a job."

Trying to suppress her frustration at the maze of answers that led to more questions, she gave up. She turned her attention to Daryn's nieces as the youngsters woke. *Grossdawdi* Christy was the last one to open his eyes, and he offered her a generous smile. The old man had always made her feel welcome when she went to Ruthie's parents' house for their quilting circle.

It took less time than she'd anticipated to get the girls ready to return to the ranch. As she did every day, Ruthie had their backpacks already packed. She made sure each of them, including Carrie, had a small bag of chocolate chunk cookies.

"I'll make sure Daryn gets some of them." Carrie glanced at the girls. "I'll have to guard them with my life from the cookie patrol."

Kayla giggled as did Rae-Rae, though she probably didn't understand what was funny. When Ella smiled, it seemed a *wunderbaar* victory, and Carrie wasn't sure if her smile or Ruthie's was broader before she led the *kinder* to the buggy she'd left in the barnyard.

Carrie's smile faded and Ella's vanished when a wagon pulled in next to the buggy and Daryn leaped down. The little girl grabbed her sister's hands, knocking their cookies to the ground. Carrie collected the bags and nodded when Ella said they'd wait in the buggy.

When she saw Daryn's grim expression, Carrie wanted to join them. Instead she stood with her hands filled with bags of cookies as he strode toward her.

"What's wrong?" she asked.

He was just as curt. "Carlos told me my sister's bishop from Missouri called *Doktor* Lynny."

"You gave the bishop the veterinarian's phone number?"

"The Marquezes suggested it because she has an answering service, which can take important messages." He took a big breath, then plunged on. "There's someone interested in the farm my sister and her husband owned."

"Isn't that *gut*?" She didn't understand why he looked more dreary than usual. Hearing shouts from the buggy, she knew she needed to get the girls to the cabin where they could exhaust their post-nap energy playing in the yard. "Wouldn't it be a relief for your family not to have that responsibility?"

"It would be, and the money left after the bills are paid off will provide a *gut* start for each of the girls when they marry."

"But?"

"But I keep asking myself how I tell them they're about to lose their final connection to their parents and brother. Everything I think of would be wrong."

"Ask Jerek to help you."

"Are you saying to have him tell them?" The tension eased in his voice.

She hated to dash his hopes, but shook her head. "No, ask Jerek to help *you* find the right words. Ask him and ask God. They'll guide you."

"I don't know what I—or anyone else—could say that will make a bit of difference. They keep losing everything they thought they'd have forever." His gaze riveted on the buggy, and his shoulders slumped.

"Words won't suffice, but let them see how sad this makes you, too."

"What *gut* will that do?"

His despair was augmented by something that sounded like frustration. What else was bothering him?

"You can't safeguard your nieces from life's sorrows and ills," she said. "I know you want to."

"I'm about to make it worse." Taking another deep breath, he said, "Putting it off won't help."

"Or will it?" When he looked at her, she said, "There's no need to tell them. You said someone was interested in the farm, but there hasn't been an offer, ain't so?"

"Not yet, but they're interested."

"Which is *gut*. However until they close on the farm, why tell the girls? Plenty of things can keep a deal from going through. Why don't you wait and see what happens? Or better yet, call the Realtor yourself. In the meantime, you can help them enjoy their memories. They'll always have those to treasure."

"What about Rae-Rae? How much will she remember?"

"Everything her sisters share with her." She could no longer keep from putting her fingers on his sleeve and tried to pay no attention to the swarm of warmth climbing her arm. "Do you think Ella will allow her to forget a single thing about their lives in Missouri?"

His answer was swallowed by a frantic scream. She felt her own rising in her throat when she saw Ella and Rae-Rae standing by the fence surrounding the bison's pasture. Both were pointing into the field, and Ella shrieked, "Kayla, *komm* back!"

Pushing past Carrie, Daryn ran to the fence. He heard Kolton calling from the house, but ignored his friend. Within seconds, he was on the other side of the fence. Knowing he mustn't spook the herd, he kept to a lope he hoped the bison would dismiss as a normal walk. He cut off Kayla, who was babbling to the animals as if they were no bigger than puppies.

He wrapped his arm around her from behind and clasped his hand over her mouth before she could squeal in surprise or protest. She wiggled until he whispered they needed to be quiet for the bison. Backing away from the herd, which hadn't glanced in their direction, except for a couple of curious calves, he didn't lower his palm from Kayla's mouth until they were on the other side of the fence.

He set the *kind* on the ground and assured Carrie and Kolton that she was unharmed. Kolton went to examine the gate to discover how the little girl had managed to open it.

"You can't go in there," Daryn said in his sternest voice.

It had as little impact on Kayla as it had on Perry. "Want to see'm. See biggest cows." Her bottom lip stuck out.

"They aren't cows. They're bison." He realized it would be useless to explain to the *kinder* that the great beasts were closer to wild animals than the domesticated cattle they knew. "They're dangerous."

"Eat little girls?" Rae-Rae's eyes widened.

"No eat Kayla." Kayla began to cry.

He wasn't prepared for Ella's fury. She gripped Kayla by the shoulders and shook her. Rae-Rae gave a soft cry of alarm as Ella pushed her face closer to Kayla's and said, "Don't leave us, too."

Rae-Rae began to howl. He scooped the sobbing toddler into his arms before pulling Kayla away from her angry sister.

"That's enough, Ella," he said.

The *kind* scowled at him. Would she retort?

Carrie stepped in. Kayla ran toward her, and she put her arm around the *kind*. Smiling, Carrie knelt and began to soothe the girls by explaining bison ate grass, not girls. How did she find the humor in every situation? Instead of being mired in his horror of seeing his niece in the field and fearing he'd let his sister down, Carrie was taking the situation in stride.

No, she wasn't calm. Her fingers were shaking, and her face had scant color. She smiled as she sent the girls to the buggy. As she came to her feet, she sighed.

"If it's okay with you," she said, straightening her bonnet, "I'm going to give Kayla a time-out when we get to the cabin. She needs to learn to obey the rules, and having to sit and not play with her sisters for fifteen minutes will be a punishment that makes her think twice next time."

"Why are you punishing her when it's my fault?"

She frowned. "Your fault? You told her *not* to go into the field."

"I should have been—"

He realized how irritated she was with him when she interrupted. "Do you think it does anyone any *gut* to have you berate yourself over every decision? So what if Kayla got into the field? She's learned not to make such a mistake again."

"But it shouldn't have happened in the first place."

"So you think you should be the perfect parent? There's only been one perfect person in history, and His name wasn't Daryn Yutzy."

He scowled. "I never said I was perfect, but I want to be a responsible guardian."

"You are!"

How Daryn wished he could believe Carrie! There wasn't a hint of doubt in her voice, but he was drowning in uncertainty. He thought of how his brother, Mark, had sought support from their family each time Daryn had embarked on another prank or round of mischief. Had Mark questioned himself as much as Daryn was now? It seemed impossible to believe because Mark had always acted as if the line between right and wrong couldn't be budged.

Yet now Daryn was acting exactly as his brother had. First with Perry and now with his nieces. He was making a mess of everything, and he didn't have any idea how to stop.

He still had none five hours later when he returned to the cabin to find the girls had been fed their evening meal and were bathed and coloring at the kitchen table. It'd been a long afternoon. He'd been glad to see, when he returned to the ranch after spending time with Kolton and the bison, that Perry had finished cleaning the stable and done other chores he'd been assigned. The teen had given him clipped answers and a lot of attitude, but when Daryn refused to be baited into an argument, Perry headed home to the Detweilers' farm.

Before coming to the cabin, Daryn had gone to the ranch office to make a call to the Missouri Realtor who informed him that, though an offer on the Byler farm was expected, it might not be until the following week.

"Or it may not come," the woman told him. "People change their minds or can't make up their minds. I'll let you know when I hear anything."

Daryn had to be satisfied with that. He was grateful he didn't yet have to tell the girls about what was happening. Carrie's advice had been right.

When he shared the information with her while she finished folding the laundry, which was stacked on the couch, she seemed to understand how the delay made him feel as if he'd dodged a stampede. "I'm glad you spoke with the Realtor."

"Me, too. *Danki*, Carrie, for the *gut* advice."

"You're—"

"Me say *danki*, too," Kayla asserted as she came over

to stand beside them. "Me sorry, *Onkel* Daryn. Me be *gut* next time, ain't so?"

He ruffled her soft hair. "*Ja*, you'll be *gut* next time. *Danki* for being a *gut* girl."

His niece gave him a big smile and skipped to the table. Turning to Carrie, he asked, "Did you coach her to say that?"

"I suggested you saved her like one of the characters in their books did for a little bird."

"What kind of character?"

"Are you sure you want to know?"

"Probably not, but tell me anyhow."

She laughed. "A grouchy bear who was awakened from hibernation by the little bird."

As Rae-Rae and Kayla giggled, he felt amusement rising in his throat. The sensation was sweet and unfamiliar after so long. It was gone like a popped soap bubble when he saw Ella's unsmiling face before she returned to her coloring.

Beside him, Carrie murmured, "She needs more time."

"For what?" He didn't give her a chance to answer as he went outside on some flimsy excuse. He thought Carrie might follow, but she didn't. Dropping into the bentwood rocker, he told himself it was for the best because he didn't have anything else to say.

Chapter Eight

The early morning knock at his door the following week startled Daryn. Carrie no longer knocked, and the kids didn't. They rushed through the door as if being chased by a wolf, crashing the door against the wall.

Pushing back from the table, he winced as he stood. He'd been shoved into a corner by a startled horse yesterday, and he had bruises to remind him how important it was to be aware of where a horse was at all times. Not that he blamed the horse, which was as gentle as an old dog. An ancient pickup had backfired outside the stable. The horse had panicked and pinned him against the stall. Just for a second, but long enough for his muscles to remember the abuse.

He stifled a groan when he reached for the door. He needed to get the knocking stopped before the noise woke the girls. His greeting went half said when he saw who stood on his porch. The woman was short, not much taller than Ruthie Lehman. Her blond hair was laced with silver and her face wrinkled.

"*Gute mariye*, Daryn," she said.

"*Gute mariye*, Alberta."

He'd seen Carrie's *mamm* on church Sundays, but hadn't done more than give her a greeting in passing on his way to join the men waiting to go into the Sunday service. The lines in her face hadn't been carved by age, but by pain.

"*Gute mariye*, Alberta." Grimacing at his unnecessary repetition, he asked, "What can I do for you? Carrie isn't here."

"I know. She's at the diner at this hour." She looked past him. "May I *komm* in?"

"*Ja*." He didn't want her to think he'd forgotten his manners, so he motioned toward the couch. "Would you like to sit?"

"*Danki*." She walked with measured steps, her shoulders hunched as if she walked against a strong wind. Sitting, she touched her forehead. Her fingers leaped away as if her skin was too hot to touch. "Forgive me. My head is pounding."

"My *aenti* suffered from migraines, so I know how awful they can be." He didn't add that he had another *aenti* who had caused more headaches in the family than he had when he was younger. "I'm sorry you're afflicted with them."

"That's kind of you to say." She gave him a smile, and for the first time, he saw the resemblance between *mamm* and daughter. "My family has picked up the slack when I can't do anything but stay in a dark and quiet room. Carrie has been a true blessing to me." Her gaze swept over him in a blatant appraisal. "And a blessing to you as well."

"*Ja*. My nieces love her." He glanced toward the bedroom door as he sat facing Alberta. Had the door been that far ajar before? He couldn't tell if three little girls were eavesdropping on them.

"I'm not surprised. She has a way with *kinder*. When she gave up her assistant teaching job to work at the diner, I suspect it broke her heart."

Though he guessed Alberta knew the true reasons her daughter had changed jobs, he wasn't going to ask. Had Carrie given up being the assistant teacher because she needed to make more money? He couldn't imagine another reason she'd left a position she must have loved. Though the Detweilers' finances weren't any of his business, he'd heard the stories of how they had suffered from a massive loss of their quinoa crops. He respected how the family was surviving through hard work and faith.

"She's been much happier since she's been spending time with your nieces," Alberta went on.

"They've been happier, too."

"What about you?"

"Me? I'm grateful Carrie has helped the girls."

"Grateful? Nothing more?"

Her gaze became more intense, and he was certain of her real reason for visiting. She'd heard how much time Carrie was spending at the ranch. The Amish grapevine was efficient, and he surmised Gerald had given the gossip an extra boost to convince Carrie to quit before she risked her reputation.

Gerald was a *dummkopf.* He should know Daryn wouldn't allow her reputation to suffer. He'd made every effort to keep from causing trouble for Carrie by having her name connected romantically with his.

"Alberta," he said, putting every ounce of sincerity in his voice, "I feel privileged to call Carrie my friend."

The older woman's face displayed nothing but pain, so he couldn't tell if she believed his assertion or not. Why should she when he wasn't sure if he believed it himself?

Carrie looked up from the small dress she was mending to the clock on the kitchen wall. Daryn should have been home a half hour ago. Something important must have delayed him, but his nieces were growing impatient for supper. There wasn't much food in the pantry or the refrigerator, and he'd told her he'd bring supplies because he had to make a run into Lost River to collect a shipment for the ranch.

At least she'd left the makings for her family's evening meal in the refrigerator at home, so *Daed* and Gerald could fend for themselves. She'd give Daryn another half hour, and then she'd go to the big house and ask *Doktor* Lynny if she could borrow items to make the girls their supper.

"Book?" asked Ella as she climbed onto the sofa beside Carrie. Her motions were clumsy because she had Freckles under one arm and a book under the other. It was the book Carrie had given her at the food truck event. Sitting next to Carrie, she settled the stuffed dog on her lap.

"This one?" Carrie asked with mock severity. "Haven't we worn out the pages reading it?"

"Not yet." A soft laugh came from the *kind*. "Read it!"

Treasuring Ella's laugh, Carrie put her mending in the basket on the floor. She made sure she closed the lid because, as she'd expected, the other two girls came running to hear the story, too. She waited while they settled on the couch before she opened the book and began to read.

She savored the glow from their faces and thanked God that they could escape from sorrow while she read the book. Maybe that was why with every rereading she found more to add to the story, using elements from the illustrations. Each of the animals on the pages had adventures that intersected with Cinderella's story. She didn't have to worry about forgetting one because the girls reminded her. The little book that had taken minutes to read now required more than a half hour. Not only the story, but the animals' sounds and actions, which sent the little girls crawling and wiggling and flapping their arms. When Carrie copied them, they began to laugh before she gathered them in a big hug.

"Looks like it's book time," came a deep voice from behind her.

As Carrie sat straighter on the sofa, Kayla and Rae-Rae

ran to Daryn who was closing the door. They flung their arms around him, talking at the same time about the story.

Ella didn't move other than to hold her hand out for the book. Giving it to her, Carrie embraced the little girl. Ella softened against her, then slid off the sofa as Daryn spoke to her sisters. She slipped into the bedroom, though she glanced back a couple of times with a wistful expression.

"She won't let herself get close to anyone," Daryn said after disentangling himself from the younger girls. He set two bags of groceries on the table. "Especially not me."

"We need to keep trying."

"I'm not giving up." He watched the other girls go into the bedroom. "Hope entrusted them with me, and I'm not going to let her down again."

He winced, and she guessed he'd said something he hadn't intended. About letting his sister down or letting her down *again*? She resisted asking. In one way, Daryn and his eldest niece were the same. The more you pushed, the faster they pulled away.

Unpacking the grocery bags, he said, "Please stay for supper. I'm late, so it's the least I can do."

"Have me make supper for you?" she teased.

"No, having us make supper together." He pushed a bag of potatoes toward her. "If you could peel those, I'll get started on everything else."

"What are we having?"

"Wait and see."

Pleased his mood had changed for the better, Carrie listened as he told about the ups and downs of dealing with deliveries in Lost River. He didn't laugh, but he had her doing so while he shared how he'd had to crawl through a pile of boxes and come face-to-face with a mouse and the cat chasing it.

"Did the cat catch it?" she asked as the potato peels fell with an easy rhythm into the composting bin.

"I'm not sure, because I don't know who was more surprised. The cat, the mouse or me." He pulled a couple of containers of leftover beef gravy from the freezer on the bottom of the refrigerator. Dumping them into a pot, he put it on the stove.

Her eyes widened when he opened a package of cheese curds. He put them into a shallow bowl while watching the gravy warm.

"What are we having?" she asked.

"Something near and dear to my taste buds." He stirred the gravy and then began to chop scallions, but didn't explain further.

When he crumbled bacon into another pan, the aroma must have reached the *kinder*, because they came to the table. Eagerness filled their eyes as Daryn asked Carrie to slice the potatoes into fries. She set them to fry.

"Are you ready to make poutine?" Daryn asked.

"Poo...?" Kayla's nose wrinkled. "Poo for dinner?"

Carrie had to look away so the little girl didn't see her grin. Her eyes met Daryn's, and when he arched his eyebrows, she choked on her suppressed laugh. Though he didn't smile, she was certain his somber expression had lightened. For him, that was a monumental change. As much as Ella needed to escape from her emotionless prison, Daryn needed to break loose from his self-imposed dreariness. Maybe tonight was the beginning of that grasp for freedom from whatever held him captive.

"Poutine," he said, then repeated with emphasis, "*Poo-teen*. It's a favorite dish in Prince Edward Island, though it came from Quebec."

The *kinder* regarded him in confusion.

"Canada, where your family is from," Carrie said, then wished she hadn't when the three little girls' bafflement cascaded into sorrow. How could she have forgotten how any mention of the *kinder*'s relatives saddened them? "It's the place where one of my favorite books is set. *Anne of Green Gables*. I loved reading those stories because Anne always used her imagination to create *wunderbaar* adventures."

"Read it to us!" Ella exclaimed. "Tonight."

Carrie's delight with the little girl's participation in the conversation became distress. How could she have forgotten that Anne Shirley, the heroine of *Anne of Green Gables*, had been an orphan sent to live with strangers?

"Not tonight," she said. "We're in the middle of our bedtime book about the dog and the cat and the mouse, remember?"

"Oh, okay." Ella's enthusiasm vanished.

Leaning toward the little girl, she whispered, "Your sisters are too little to enjoy it. Let's wait until they're big like you."

Ella nodded and scrambled from her chair when Carrie sent the youngsters to wash up before they ate.

With a sigh, Carrie picked up the coloring books and stacked them in a box by the stairs to the loft. She went into the kitchen to get what she needed to set the table. She reached for plates, but Daryn told her to get bowls instead.

"Are you all right?" he asked, staying near the stove to keep an eye on the frying potatoes. "You look upset."

"I shouldn't have mentioned *Anne of Green Gables*. Ella will want to have it read to her." She got five bowls. "It's not easy finding books that won't upset them. I never realized how many orphans are in stories. Or twins. The Bobbsey Twins books were favorites for me when I was Ella's age."

"You can't read those books to them. Not now."

"I know." She looked at where the girls were splashing water in the bathroom. She would sop it up before putting them to bed. "But, on the other hand, we can't tiptoe around their grief."

"I've been trying."

"I have, too, but it's impossible. That grief is a part of them."

His fists tightened at his sides. "I keep praying they'll put it behind them and move on."

"They'll move on, but the grief will never go completely." She took a deep breath before forcing herself to continue, "It's a complicated dance between our hearts and grief. We want to push it away. It wants to cling to us. Fighting it adds to our pain, so we have to learn to balance it."

"But you haven't." His eyes narrowed so she couldn't tell if his words were sympathetic or accusatory.

"No, I haven't." She tried not to think of nearly two years of mornings when waking and seeing Bethany's empty bed on the other side of the room sucked her breath from her.

"So how do you expect little kids to?"

"By continuing to live as their parents would have wished them to. It's what I try to do each day. Live my life as I would have if Bethany had never vanished."

"You're living a lie."

"No, I'm trying to live my life. I can't forget my twin is gone." She looked to where Ella was watching her younger sisters drying their hands while she waited her turn. "But I can remember my future is ahead of me, and I can make it whatever I want. *Ja*, the grief will never let me go, but some days I can forget it for an hour or two at a time. I count that as a victory."

"A small victory."

"But to misquote our bishop who always says a small blessing is still a blessing, a small victory—"

"Is still a victory." He sighed. "Okay, I get it, but that doesn't make anything easier."

"I never said it did. All it does is make the pain bearable some of the time."

How Daryn wanted that to be true! To let go of his guilt and his self-incrimination would be a blessing, but he'd failed. Or, more often, got into another mess.

Carrie believed what she was saying. Yet had her faith that everything would become better helped her deal with her private pain? He had to wonder if it was worse to hide the truth behind a smile than behind a frown.

He pushed aside his dispiriting thoughts as his nieces ran to the table. Carrie got them settled while he drained the fries and the bacon. He put them on two different platters. Bringing them to the table, he got cheese and scallions while she poured glasses of *millich*. The gravy continued to bubble on the stove.

"Poo?" asked Rae-Rae as she gripped the edge of the table and leaned forward to get a better view.

He lowered his head for silent grace, and the girls and Carrie followed suit. It felt strange to be the one who set the length of time for the prayers. He'd gone so quickly from a footloose cowboy to the head of a family. *Lord, help me do what's right for these three little girls who depend on me.* It was a huge ask because he spent most days making mistakes. The one thing he'd gotten right was asking Carrie to watch his girls.

Looking through his half-closed eyes to where she sat with her head lowered, one hand on Rae-Rae's arm to keep the littlest one from reaching for the food before they thanked God for it, he admired the gentle curve of her cheek and her chin that could be lifted in a stubborn pose in the blink of an eye. She exuded warmth and happiness while she fought her sorrow. He wondered if he'd ever met a stronger person.

He raised his head and cleared his throat. As four sets of eyes aimed at him, he explained that poutine was a simple but delicious dish of French fries topped with the other ingredients. "The best part is if you don't want something on the table, you don't have to have it. Poutine can be anything you want as long as it has fries, cheese and gravy. Be careful. Everything is hot, but take what you want. Fries on the bottom, then the toppings and the gravy last."

Daryn had never seen the girls so engaged with anything he suggested. How each *kind* arranged her poutine in her shallow bowl revealed so much about what he'd learned of her personality. Little Rae-Rae dumped handfuls of cheese on top of her fries and giggled as pieces bounced off onto the table where she could scoop them up and drop them again. Kayla arranged her curds across the mound of fries, making the bowl look pretty and appetizing. In contrast, Ella, who was working next to Carrie, had a presentation as precise as if she'd counted the number of curds to place on each side of the pile of fries.

When he looked up, he guessed his concern at how Ella was maintaining her tight control was visible because Carrie frowned and shook her head. Did she think he would comment to the *kind* about her choices? Carrie glanced from him to the little girl's bowl, then took a handful of the remaining cheese curds and made a happy face on her fries.

"Poutine makes me smile," she said, turning her plate so the *kinder* could see it.

"You haven't tasted it yet." He tried to play into her upbeat mood in a desperate attempt to draw Ella into having fun, too.

"Who says?" Carrie popped a fry and curds into her mouth after scooping up bacon and a piece of scallion. "Yummy."

That brought hearty laughs from the younger girls and a softer chuckle from Ella. He wanted to capture that faint sound and treasure it.

All he could do was say, "You haven't tasted the best part yet."

"The best part?" she asked.

"The gravy." He returned to the stove. After turning off the burner, he lifted the pot and carried it to the table. He set it on a trivet. Wagging a warning finger, he said, "This is hot, so stay back while I put it on your poutine."

No one spoke as he ladled the gravy, letting it drizzle over the fries. He watched their faces until Carrie yelped that gravy was pouring over the side of a plate. He turned his attention to what he was doing.

"Dig in," he urged as he put down the pot. "But be careful. It's very hot."

He swirled a fry through the gravy and melting cheese. Holding it up, he blew on it. That brought giggles from the younger girls and a laugh from Carrie. Ella smiled at his clowning.

Wiping more gravy from her bowl, Carrie said, "This is *wunderbaar*. I'm going to serve this on my food truck."

"I'll be your first customer."

"No, me!" Kayla jumped up and down.

"Me! Me!" Rae-Rae echoed.

Gratitude blared through his skull as Ella added her voice to the excitement. When his gaze collided with Carrie's across the table, he knew, for the first time in longer than he could recall, he was where he was supposed to be. The sensation wouldn't last long because doubts and guilt would flood over him, but he was going to appreciate it for as long as it lasted.

Chapter Nine

When Carrie didn't collect her things and leave once supper was done, Daryn was surprised. She offered to clean up after their fun meal of poutine. The table was covered with fingerprints in melted cheese and gravy. She found ways for his nieces to help while he stored the oil used for frying the potatoes in the freezer. Threading his way between the *kinder*, he thanked each when she brought him a used utensil or bowl.

Once the kitchen was spotless, he was impressed nothing had been dropped and broken. The girls were yawning and rubbing their eyes. Having them assist calmed them because Carrie had led them in childish songs that sounded like lullabies. Were they the ones she'd sung to his nieces when he arrived home after they'd gone to bed? The gentle melodies brought a quiet end to a busy day.

"Can I help you tuck them in?" Carrie asked as she wiped her hands on a dish towel and hung it over the rack by the sink.

He nodded, not trusting himself to speak. If he did, he might ask her to stay longer. Tonight, like most of the times they'd spent time together, they'd been focused on his nieces. He wished the two of them could steal an hour—or longer—by themselves. Every time they were alone, either his nieces rushed to them or her brother materialized like a fairy-tale phantom.

"*Danki*, Daryn. I'd enjoy that." She glanced at the girls and a mischievous smile twitched. "After they have a bedtime story or two or three with us."

The *kinder* cheered, even Ella, though as always her reaction was more muted than her exuberant sisters.

"That sounds like fun," he said. "They love when you read to them."

"No," Carrie said.

No? She was turning down her invitation for him to join them? He scowled as the girls exchanged uneasy glances.

"You are going to read to them," she added.

"Me?"

"Why not? They would love to have you read to them."

He was astonished how much pleasure rushed through him at the thought of sharing a book with the girls. But could he emulate Carrie's easy ability to bring a character to life with no more than an inflection of her voice?

Carrie didn't give him time to worry about that as she herded him along with the girls into the downstairs bedroom where two beds and Rae-Rae's crib took up most of the space. More quickly than he could, she had them changed into their nightgowns, their teeth brushed and a glass of water for each of them.

Going into the main room, he got a chair which he set between the two beds. The younger girls edged closer. Ella clambered up on the bed as well, but remained near where Carrie stood at the foot. A soft sigh of relief slipped past his lips, and he had to admit to himself how unsure he'd been if his oldest niece would participate. The little girl leaned against Carrie, who put an arm around her at the same time. Carrie motioned for him to begin and that sense of being where he belonged rushed through him. It was so unfamiliar he savored it. He wasn't sure how long he would have sat there, lost in something akin to happiness, if Kayla hadn't nudged him.

"Read our story, *Onkel* Daryn," she ordered.

"Read!" echoed the eager Rae-Rae.

With a smile, he did. The story was about two kittens and a puppy who got into mischief. As the younger girls laughed and Ella smiled, he found himself becoming the characters, meowing and barking.

He closed the book with a sigh, then rose to help Carrie tuck each girl into her bed. She received hugs and kisses. He didn't get the same, but the younger girls gave him smiles before they turned over to fall asleep.

When Carrie turned off the lamp and left the door ajar so a narrow shaft of light flowed in, Daryn expected her to bid him a *gut nacht* and be on her way. Instead she sat on the couch and waited for him to join her. He guessed she had something she wanted to say to him.

Gut, because he had something to say to her. "*Danki*," he said, choosing the rocking chair that faced the sofa. "I didn't realize what I've been missing."

"They want you in their lives, Daryn." Happiness glowed in her eyes. "You're the thread in their lives that ties them to the past and the family they've lost."

"A thread that's been ready to snap." He rubbed his brow.

"It's not a single thread. There are multiple strands made up of all of you." She shook her head, and he watched in fascination as a soft tendril fell forward to curl along her cheek.

She brushed it back before he could give in to his yearning to do the same. His fingers fisted on the arms of the rocking chair. Without her help, he'd have been lost when it came to taking care of the girls. He might not have thought of asking Ruthie to watch them in the morning while Carrie was at the diner. Before Carrie had been invited by his nieces into their lives, he'd been sinking beneath the weight of grief and fear. He'd watched as she'd treated the three girls with kindness and invited them to be regular kids, not three little mourners.

"No," she continued, "it's not a thread. It's a rubber band. No matter how much you stretch that connection, it draws you back together."

"Unless it snaps."

"You're not going to let that happen."

He heard her sadness and knew she was wondering if the thread between her and her twin sister had broken. He was amazed how this woman carried her load of grief and uncertainty while offering the world a smile and a pleasant word. She was unlike anyone he'd met. Strong, yet gentle. Determined, yet able to bend. Beautiful with those lips that looked so kissable.

When she spoke, telling him Kayla had scraped her knee and he should check it in the morning before dropping off the girls at the Lehman farm, he pushed aside his thoughts which urged him to risk everything he and the girls needed so he could have the kiss he wanted so desperately.

Had he lost his mind? It had been less than a day since her *mamm* had asked him if he had any feelings in addition to gratitude for Carrie. He considered telling Carrie that Alberta had stopped by, but halted himself. What *gut* would that do? She already was being shadowed by her brother. She didn't need to be burdened by knowing her *mamm* was checking on her, too.

"Did you pick that book I read tonight on purpose?" he asked, cutting her off mid-word.

Her eyes narrowed as they searched his. "On purpose? I'm not sure what you mean."

"I mean you chose a story about young animals who made a lot of mistakes."

As she laughed, her face cleared. "Daryn, look through the girls' storybooks. A *gut* portion are about learning from mistakes. A story that teaches and entertains at the same time is the best sort of book." She didn't pause as she added, "What made you think I chose that book on purpose?"

He was about to avoid the question as he had so many others. It had become a habit to be evasive. Tonight, he wanted to be honest and take the chance she wouldn't judge him as others had. That she would see that while he owned what had been his fault, he didn't want to be burdened with what hadn't.

"Because I thought you were trying to help me, too," he said. "To realize it's possible to become a better person after messing up."

"You haven't messed up here, Daryn."

"No, but I did before I got here. Sometimes on my own and sometimes with others. Sometimes it was my doing, but not always."

"What do you mean?"

As he saw compassion in her eyes, he didn't hesitate to say, "In Wyoming, there was a girl. Not a girl. A young woman. A young *Englischer* woman who was trouble."

Carrie's eyes widened. "A young woman in trouble?"

He shook his head as he waved aside her words. "Not *in trouble*. Just trouble."

"I don't understand."

"Nor do I any longer. There was an attraction there, but it wasn't like I wanted her for a girlfriend. She was *Englisch*, and I had no interest in leaving a plain life, such as it was when I was there. The nearest plain community was hours away by car, but I continued to walk the path I believed the Lord set for me."

"Except for this woman."

He nodded. "I think, looking back, I was intrigued by someone who got into more messes than I did."

She pulled her feet up beneath her on the sofa. "You may be surprised when I say this, but I get why you felt that way. Sometimes you need to have someone to stand beside who makes you feel *gut* about yourself."

"There are other ways than trying to stand beside the most flawed person you can find."

"You haven't made the same mistake here." Her smile returned. "If you had, Gerald would have informed me right away."

He let her *gut* humor erode his despair. "I don't doubt that. Your brother is doing his best to make sure you don't stand within a mile of any miscreant." Knowing he might be treading where he shouldn't go, but hoping she'd be as open with her pain as he'd been with his, he said, "Everyone says you and your sister look alike."

"Our features are the same." She didn't seem put off by his comment, and he was surprised when she went on, "There's one big difference. She's more than six inches shorter than I am. Not much taller than Ruthie. My earliest memories are of people admiring Bethany's doll-like appearance and then seeing me, gangly and too tall. A *kind* notices when her sister is called *adorable* and she's labeled as *sturdy*."

"Plain people said those things?"

"*Ja*. We're taught about how the outer part of us isn't as important as the inner. However, that gets forgotten. You must have seen that."

"Especially when young men get together to discuss which girl they should ask to ride home in their buggy after a youth event."

When the twinkle returned to her eyes, stripping away the shadows of pain that always dimmed them whenever she spoke of her sister, he thanked God for helping him choose the right words. He was more grateful when she agreed to stay for a cup of tea before heading home. It was going to be the best evening he'd had since before he'd arrived in Wyoming and had his life almost ruined forever.

"Red alert."

Carrie paused at the whisper from the diner's other waitress, Paige Jenkins. She edged closer to the soda dispenser around the corner from the long counter where Paige, who was a decade older than Carrie, stood. Her friend worked a later shift than Carrie, coming on about an hour before Carrie left. Paige worked long hours, but never hesitated to agree to move Greenie Gal where it needed to go.

"What's up?" Carrie asked.

The woman whose dark hair was beginning to show strands of silver narrowed her hazel eyes. She put her hands on the waist of the half-apron she wore over T-shirt and jeans. "It's them."

"Them who?"

"Three of the nastiest of Snow White's dwarfs. Gloomy and Bossy and Annoying."

Carrie laughed. Paige's nicknames could have left her in trouble if their boss, Lou Spanos, overheard. Despite that, Paige continued to label each of their regulars with a name that might have made them chuckle or gotten her fired.

Carrie, on the other hand, appreciated the code, which allowed her to know who was in the diner without a customer overhearing their name. She took a deep breath to prepare herself. Her older brother, Gerald, was known as "Bossy" so he must have been in the diner. Her brother came in often, but Daryn, whom Paige called "Grouchy," and Perry, who was "Annoying" in Paige-speak, seldom dined there.

"Do you want me to wait on them?" Paige asked.

"What's the point? Gerald will insist on seeing me."

Paige grimaced. "Does he think you're going to run off with a cowboy during the lunch rush? He should know by now that, if you were stupid enough to do that, Lou would hunt you down and make sure you finished your shift."

Her friend's jesting made Carrie feel better. Lou was as gentle as a spring breeze. Though let someone try to mess with one of her staff or complain about her *kaffi*, and the white-haired woman could become an attack dog.

"I'll handle him and the others," Carrie said.

"Thanks. I need to get the orders in the window or Lou will have my hide." She started to turn, then paused. "Carrie, did you remember to bring those recipes for the burger sauces you created for your food trailer?"

Reaching into her apron, she pulled out several slips of paper. "I remembered to bring them, but did I remember to give them to you? No!" Laughing, she handed the recipes to her friend. "Realize what I wrote are guesstimates. You know I never measure anything."

"At least these are starting points." She glanced at the slips. "Turmeric? No wonder I couldn't figure what I was missing. My kids will be impressed I can make the sauce they've been begging for."

"Paige! Food up!" came Lou's voice from the kitchen.

Stuffing the pages into her apron pocket, Paige rushed to serve the food before it got cold.

Taking a deep breath and putting on a smile, Carrie went

into the dining room. She couldn't dampen her curiosity about why Daryn and her brother and cousin were at the diner together. Usually Daryn and Gerald gave each other a wide berth, and Perry didn't enjoy being with either.

When she came around the corner, all became clear. Gerald was perched on a stool at the counter by himself. Perry was following Daryn, but they weren't alone. Paige hadn't mentioned the girls were with Daryn. Carrie watched as he maneuvered the double stroller between the tables. Ella walked beside it, clutching the handle as if she were about to yank it away. Their procession was as somber as a funeral until Kayla climbed out of the stroller and burst around a table. She didn't walk. She skipped, whirling, dancing, taking the longest route between two points. Her fingers trailed along the side of the tables, following the grooves cut into the edging. With a giggle, she rushed across the room and stared at the jukebox's blinking lights. She tried to catch each pulse and laughed when they eluded her.

"Pretty!" she announced, eliciting smiles and chuckles from the other customers.

Except for Gerald, who was scowling at the little family.

Wanting to tell him he wasn't daunting anyone with his vexed expression, Carrie went to greet the girls. They gave her enthusiastic hugs, and Daryn nodded when she asked if he needed one high chair or two. He held up one finger while trying to corral Kayla, who was going from table to table to speak to everyone. Most of the customers wouldn't understand *Deitsch*, but that didn't slow her. She got smiles and waves before Carrie grasped her by the shoulders and steered her to the others.

While Paige got the high chair, Carrie went to the counter and took her brother a cup of *kaffi*.

"The usual, Gerald?" she asked, not letting her eyes stray

toward where Daryn was settling Rae-Rae into a high chair while Kayla scrambled up onto a booster seat that Paige had brought as well. The other waitress began to take their order.

Perry rose and sat next to Gerald. He must consider her brother better than Daryn, who would have talked to him about work. Gerald flashed him a frown and gave his order to Carrie. She wasn't sure why. He had the same cheese, peppers and bacon omelet, sourdough toast and orange juice each time he came in. Perry ordered a chicken salad club and fries. She almost told her cousin about the poutine Daryn had taught them to make yesterday, but she could imagine her brother exploding with fury that she'd lingered so late at the ranch last night.

Giving their orders to Lou, she looked over at where Daryn sat with his girls. She went to the stack of booster seats and picked up a second one. She took it to the booth. Not giving Ella a chance to argue, she set it on the bench. "It's your size."

"I'm not a *boppli*." The girl gave her the scowl she usually reserved for her *onkel*.

"No, you're not, but you're going to spill your delicious meal if you have to reach up that high. You don't want to miss any of your..."

"French toast," Daryn supplied. "They're having French toast."

"Sounds yummy."

"I thought I'd drop the girls off if you don't mind," he said. "Ruthie was called in to work."

Carrie's stomach dropped. Her friend was a native speaker interpreter for the Rio Grande County courts, which meant someone who spoke *Deitsch* but not much English needed help in being understood during an interrogation.

That would mean a *kind* as young as the ones sitting with Daryn.

"Ruthie said she thinks it's because of a robbery at the feedstore last week," he hurried to say. "The cops want to talk to witnesses."

"That's got to be scary for any *kinder*."

"Scary," Rae-Rae repeated and sank into her chair.

"Super scary," Kayla whispered, staring past Carrie, while her older sister said, "Super-super scary."

Carrie looked over her shoulder. She hid her shock when she realized they were looking at her brother, who stood right behind her. Facing him, she asked in her coldest voice, "Do you need something, Gerald?"

"A refill of my *kaffi* would be nice."

Raising her hand, she gestured toward Paige in the sign language they'd perfected after years of working together. "It's on its way."

"But you're my waitress. Not Paige."

"After all the time you've spent at this diner, Gerald, I'm surprised you haven't seen how Paige and I work together. Look. She's pouring your *kaffi*."

Gerald sputtered, then turned on his heel and stamped to the stool where he sat so hard she was surprised it didn't collapse under him. He didn't pick up his cup. Just stared at her.

"Sorry about that," Daryn said.

"Don't worry. I'm used to Gerald's temper tantrums. He'll stomp around for a while. He might cackle like an angry chicken, too, but I've heard it before." She stepped aside as Paige brought a tray with their meals.

Her smile returned when she saw Daryn had ordered a hot beef sandwich with fries. She had no doubt he'd be dipping those fries in the gravy and sharing them with his nieces.

That smile slipped when she saw how the girls chatted with him instead of around him as they had a day or two ago. Last night, she and Daryn had discussed connections, and she could imagine the invisible one growing between him and the *kinder*. It would weave more tightly as the days passed, creating the pattern that would make them a family. It was everything she'd prayed for, but she couldn't help wondering how much longer there would be a place in their lives for her. Would she continue to be welcome within the heart of this new family, or would she be left behind as she'd been when Bethany went away?

Chapter Ten

Daryn pulled on his church shoes the following Sunday morning and grimaced. When he'd been at the diner with his nieces, Gerald had returned to their table and invited Daryn to join the youth group after church services this evening. He'd been so shocked at how Gerald had treated him as a fellow human being rather than a predator after his sister. He hadn't noticed then that Gerald had been miserly with details of what the youth group planned for the afternoon and evening. If they were playing ball, he'd have to find somewhere to put his shoes so they weren't scuffed beyond recovery.

Or maybe he shouldn't attend. He hadn't before. He couldn't help being curious why Gerald had extended an invitation. Maybe Gerald wanted to introduce him to a young woman who wasn't his sister.

Daryn snorted in derision. Gerald Detweiler was no matchmaker. Quite the opposite.

"Ready for church?" he called.

Ella, Kayla and Rae-Rae burst into the living room. He'd spent an hour getting their hair brushed into braids, and Ella was the only one with both intact. He did his best to get them neat. Rae-Rae's *schlupp schotzli* was wrinkled, but he didn't have time to press the white organdy. The bibbed apron would have to do.

After they'd reached the Lehman farm where church was being held, he handed over his buggy to one of the boys parking them and taking care of the horses. He paused long enough to make sure the chalk mark they made on the black buggy matched the one on his horse's flank. He'd been in a hurry once and hadn't paused to check. That Sunday in Indiana, the horse and buggy had been marked wrong, and he'd had to wait until everyone else left before he'd been able to get the buggy he'd borrowed from a friend.

He put his finger to his lips. "Quiet for God, ain't so?"

The girls remembered his admonition until they saw Carrie. They rushed to her, chattering like a tree filled with songbirds. She gave him a quick wave, then guided his nieces into the circle of women and *kinder* who welcomed them with kind smiles. Kayla, as always the first to respond, began chattering. Rae-Rae bounced at her side, no doubt copying what her older sister was saying and doing. Shy Ella hung back, close to Carrie, who put her hand on the little girl's shoulder.

"It takes time."

At the quiet words, Daryn turned to discover Noah Frye behind him. The house where Daryn was living with his nieces had once been used by Noah and his two *kinder*. With a shudder, Daryn recalled how Noah had lost his wife and how he, too, had taken a long journey with his kids to the San Luis Valley. Married to Kolton's sister, Mollie, he made his living painting barn quilts. The family moved around the valley while he completed projects.

"Time?" he repeated.

"To heal and to *komm* to terms with what won't be." Sorrow drifted through Noah's voice. "It's not just grieving for those who are gone, but for the dreams of a future with them that have died, too."

"How long does it take?" He realized he was asking as much for himself as for the girls.

"I wish I could give you a definite number, that I could say everything will be fine by this time some specific number of days, weeks, months, years from now."

"Years?"

Noah gave him a sympathetic smile. "A year is but the blink of an eye to God. What's in our hearts, whether it's joy or grief, is measured on His time, not ours."

"Listen to Noah," said Kolton as he joined them. A faint smile crinkled his eyes. "It's *gut* practice for him when he goes into the lot and is selected as our next ordained man."

"You know I can't be around Lost River enough to do that."

"We'll need a new deacon when Elroy moves with his family to Montana."

"Might as well keep him on as the deacon as ask God to give me the job. I'm not going to be here much more than he will with this new project I've got beginning near Dashtown this summer."

Daryn listened to the men. They were more like brothers than brothers-in-law. Or maybe not. He and his brother had seldom seen eye-to-eye, and their words had been aimed more at cutting than bringing them closer with *gut* humor.

Excusing himself, he went to look for Perry. He had a job to discuss with Carrie's cousin. A job, he guessed, Perry would truly enjoy. Kolton needed help separating the bison calves from the herd so the cows could be bred again. It would take more than Kolton and Daryn to accomplish the job. Kolton's brother, Tyler, had volunteered for one day to shut the sports equipment store in Lost River he managed, and Daryn had said he'd talk to Perry.

He didn't find the teen before the service started, and a quick glance around the barn where the service was being held revealed Perry wasn't attending church that day. Hoping the boy wasn't off doing something irresponsible, he tried to pay attention to the bishop's messages.

His thoughts kept wandering, pulled back each time the *Leit* stood to sing or kneeled in prayer. He focused his prayers on Perry and on his nieces and Carrie. He fought to keep his eyes from shifting to the far end of the benches on the women's side where she sat with Ella. The younger girls must have gone into the house where those too little to sit through the long service would have quiet lessons and games. He was surprised Ella hadn't gone, too, because she often refused to be separated from her sisters. When her head bobbed before she rested in Carrie's lap, he was grateful his niece was enough at peace that she was able to nap. She roused when everyone stood for the final blessing and the day's last hymn.

Though he wanted to talk to Carrie and confirm where the girls were, he was commandeered by a group of men who were stacking benches to make tables for the communal meal. He ended up sitting with Kolton and Tyler, listening to the two brothers debate a small detail of firefighting.

"You should think about volunteering, Daryn," Tyler said. "We can always use extra hands."

"And arms and strong spines." Kolton pressed his hand to his back and faked a groan. "The training will test every bit of you."

"It's meant to be team-building."

"Or team-breaking."

"The same thing."

Daryn tuned them out as he ate his sandwich and enjoyed a cool glass of lemonade. It wasn't as delicious as Carrie's, but it was what he needed on the hot sunny afternoon. Though he usually took his leave right after the meal, using the girls needing a nap as his excuse, he'd agreed to leave the *kinder* with Ruthie while he transported younger members of the youth group to a farm south of the county line near La Jara. The trip would take an hour each way, and parents wanted to make sure the newer members didn't get lost.

He was surprised when he arrived at his buggy several hours later to find Carrie sitting inside along with three teenage girls who must be around the same age as Perry. They were prattling and primping. At the sight, he almost ran into the Lehman house to spend the evening with his friends, their *kinder* and his nieces. An arched eyebrow aimed in his direction by Carrie kept him from fleeing.

More than once on the long trip, he tried to start a conversation with Carrie. Each time one of the girls interrupted with a squeal of excitement when one boy's or another's name was mentioned. As the sun dropped toward the San Juan Mountains, he began to wonder if Gerald had set up this arrangement to make sure his and Carrie's ears were ringing by the time they got to the gathering.

Daryn stepped from the buggy so the girls could slip past him. They each thanked him for the ride but never stopped their silly debate about boys whose eyes they wanted to catch. As they hurried into the house, Daryn rested his arm on the buggy. He looked across to where Carrie sat. She didn't move except for a widening grin.

"I had no idea how much teen girls talked about teen boys," he said.

Sliding out on the other side, she met him behind the

buggy. "No more than teen boys talk about teen girls at that age, I assume."

"I assume as well."

"You never talked about girls?"

"Not that I'm going to admit to."

She laughed. "Was that a joke, Daryn Yutzy? An actual joke?"

For the first time in longer than he could recall, he wished he could join her in that carefree sound. Her laughter lilted through his days like sunshine after a cloudy day, warm and refreshing. Did she have any idea how it warmed his heart that had been encased in ice for too long?

A large form stepped from the shadows. Daryn had been curious how long it would take Gerald to show up. Without a word, Carrie's brother motioned for them to follow him into the house. Carrie said nothing when Daryn looked at her, and she walked after her brother.

Daryn almost jumped into his buggy so he could return to Lost River and his nieces, but he would be expected to give the giggle contingent and Carrie a ride home unless someone else offered. It was going to be a long evening.

The room was filled with voices urging on the final participants of a game where an orange had to be passed from one person to the next without using any hands. Carrie had tried, but let the orange drop when the young man next to her had breathed taco breath in her face as he bent to catch the orange she'd been holding under her chin. Someone had handed her a glass of lemonade but it was too weak for her taste. She didn't want to leave it on a table because it might get knocked onto one of the rag rugs scattered across the floor. Maybe while everyone's eyes were on the game she could slip into the kitchen and flush it down the sink.

She turned and collided with Daryn. Lemonade splashed from her glass, hitting his shirt between his black suspenders. "Oh, my! I'm sorry."

He pulled out a blue kerchief and dabbed at the lemonade dripping between the buttons. "Don't worry. I'll rinse it off."

"Let me help you."

There must have been more desperation in her voice than she'd intended because he stared at her, then nodded. When he walked toward the kitchen at the rear of the house, she followed, edging around the crowd that was getting more excited by the game.

In the kitchen, she went to the sink. She wet a paper towel and handed it to Daryn. "Use this. I'm sorry."

"It was an accident." He shrugged his shoulders. "At least it'll give me a story to tell tomorrow."

"That sounds as if you're not having any fun. I saw you watching the games. You couldn't look more uncomfortable if you tried. Are you worried about your nieces?"

"No. I know they're having a *gut* time with Ruthie and her kids."

"They're having a *wunderbaar* time, Daryn. Ruthie is planning to let them help her mix up the cinnamon rolls tonight for tomorrow's breakfast. They'll get to make a mess tonight and have a special treat tomorrow when you drop them off." She met his eyes and wished she could find words to reassure him. "You know how much they love to spend time with Benny and Tianna."

"I know Kayla and Rae-Rae do, but Ella…" He sighed.

"She and Tianna love picture books, so they sit together and turn the pages. Sometimes, Tianna will tell her stories based on the illustrations."

"Does Ella make up stories, too?"

"Not yet." She put gentle fingers on his arm, but drew

them back when her heart threatened to bounce from her chest. "She needs more time."

"Noah said that, too."

"I'm glad he's talked to you about how he helped his *kinder* deal with their grief while he had to *komm* to terms with his. He's got a deep well of wisdom that has people whispering he might be put into the lot the next time there's an opening."

"Kolton mentioned that, but Noah reminded him that as much as he travels for his work, that could be a problem."

"There's a solution for every dilemma."

"You believe that?"

"*Ja*," she replied, not taking the bait of his scoffing words. "I trust God can see what I can't, and He'll bring the answer."

"In His time." Frustration had slipped into his voice.

"All we can do is have faith He's listening to our prayers and our hearts."

"I don't doubt that." He gave a deep sigh. "I hope I have patience to wait for His answer. It hurts to hear Kayla and Rae-Rae crying in their sleep."

"Not Ella?"

He shook his head. "When I check on them, she's comforting her sisters and is as stoic as a first responder."

In spite of herself, she smiled. "It sounds as if the kids aren't the only thing you and Noah and Kolton talked about. Is Kolton trying to recruit you for the fire department?"

"He mentioned it."

She laughed. "He asks everyone. Doesn't matter if you're male or female."

"You?"

"*Ja*, but Ruthie told him to stop trying to make me feel

guilty when I was already doing more by bringing food from the diner to feed volunteers than I could holding a hose."

"What about your brother?" He gestured to where Gerald stood in the doorway between the kitchen and the front room, his gaze riveted on the two of them.

"I'm sure he was asked, but he's never shown any interest in joining."

"Too busy keeping an eye on you, ain't so?"

She chuckled again. "He believes it's the job God has given him. He—" She halted when Gerald froze, then sticking his hand in his pocket, rushed through the crowded living room and out the main door. "If I had half a brain, I'd make my escape now."

"What?" Puzzlement added a boyish charm to his usual somber face.

"Gerald will be too busy for the next fifteen or twenty minutes to watch me."

"How do you know?"

She gave him a conspiratorial smile. "My big brother thinks he's *gut* at keeping secrets, but he forgets where he's put his cell phone. He's constantly looking for it. I'll ask him what he's lost, and he always says that it's nothing important. However, he's searching like a squirrel at winter's end trying to find the last nut it buried."

Daryn shook his head. "I can't imagine your brother as a squirrel. He's big and lumbering, not small and skittish."

"Okay. He's like a giant squirrel trying to find its last nut. Better?"

"I don't think so. The idea of a giant squirrel is upsetting at best."

She laughed, then leaned forward to whisper, "He has a girlfriend."

"He told you?"

"No. I've found his phone a couple of times in the laundry when he's left it in his pocket. The first time he did that, it almost went in the washer, but fell on the floor. Since then, I check his pockets every time I do laundry."

"So you can peek at his phone?"

"No! I can't be annoyed with him for intruding in my life if I do the same to him. Sometimes the phone blinks on to a text page, and I see the messages between him and a girl."

"A plain girl or an *Englischer*?"

"I haven't read them, but her name at the top of the page is Phoneygirl."

His blue eyes widened in shock. "Do you think your brother would walk out with an *Englischer* after Bethany jumped the fence with one?"

"Nobody knows for sure if Bethany went with an *Englischer.*"

"But you saw her with one several times before she left?"

"*Ja.*" Her shoulders sagged.

"If you believe that, your brother does, too." He rested his hand on the counter. "But will his heart heed his head? He could be getting involved with an *Englisch* woman while he's scolding you for as much as talking to one at the diner."

Carrie folded her arms in front of her and looked past Daryn toward the living room where another game was underway. It required the young men and women to work together toward a common goal. They were having fun, and she wanted to have some, too. Not with the whole group, but with the man standing in front of her.

Without a word, she opened the back door and left. She held her breath, hoping he'd follow. When she heard the faint sound of the hinges as the door reopened, she raised her eyes to the stars breaking through the indigo sky to accompany Venus on its dance across the heavens. She thanked God.

Daryn came to stand beside her, then leaned forward to rest his hands on the railing that was covered with loose paint. He straightened, shook tiny pieces off his palms, then slanted forward again.

"So are you sneaking away?" he asked.

"I need some fresh air. I thought maybe I'd walk around a bit."

"Do you want some company?"

She couldn't ignore how her heart raced at the question. To be with him alone without her brother or his kids or the rest of the world was an exhilarating thought. She held out her hand, delighting in bending the rules. There wasn't anything in their *Ordnung* that said a man and a woman couldn't hold hands, but it was an unspoken rule a man should make the first move. If she was going to break one convention, why not another?

Her hand hung in the air for what seemed like an eternity, then his slipped around hers. He drew her closer. When his fingers splayed across her cheek, she couldn't keep her gaze from settling on his lips. Oh, how she wished he would kiss her!

He murmured something she couldn't catch over the frantic throbbing of her pulse. His eyes seemed to be mapping every inch of her face, and she wanted to ask what he sought. Speaking such a simple question was beyond her as her breath matched his, sharp and quick.

The door opened, and Carrie dropped his hand and stepped aside. A head popped around the door as a guy asked if someone whose name she couldn't discern past her thundering heartbeat was with them. When Daryn said no, the kid went inside, leaving them to the night and the stars.

Grabbing her hand again, Daryn said, "*Komm mol*. Let's go before someone else intrudes."

Though every morsel of her being wanted to shout, "*Ja!*" *gut* sense had caught up with her. "I can't go without letting Gerald know where I am. He'd be furious." She leaned against the railing. "I'm sorry, but it'll be better if I stay here."

"And not make a mad dash away from your big brother?"

Hearing the regret in his voice, she wanted to reassure him that she would have loved to have time alone—the two of them—a precious commodity they'd seldom had. She swallowed the words, unsure.

"The only mad dash I'm making," she said, ensuring her voice was light, but having to change the subject before she let her yearning to be alone with him make her do something stupid, "is taking my food trailer to Dashtown arts festival. I plan to serve poutine then, but I'll be varying your recipe."

"That's no surprise." His shoulders eased from their taut pose as he rested on the railing beside her. "You like to put your touch on your menu items. What do you have in mind?"

"I'm formulating, so you're going to have to wait and see." She gave him a smile. Not a steady one, but the best she could manage. "Sometimes when I'm tossing together ingredients, I'm not sure what I'll have until it's finished."

"That's no way to develop a menu if you want to put a cookbook together."

"A cookbook?" She frowned. "What makes you think I want to write a cookbook?"

"I heard you talking to Paige the other day about recipes and how important it was that they didn't get lost or forgotten."

"I was talking about Lou's recipes."

"But isn't it as true for your recipes?"

"First I'd have to figure out what I put in them. Nobody buys a cookbook with no measurements in it."

"But you don't cook that way. I've watched you cook for the girls. You judge by smell and taste what's the right amount."

"Which is why I don't have real recipes." She patted his hand on the rail beside her, making sure her fingers didn't linger. "*Danki*, Daryn, for thinking that I might have the ability to put together a cookbook."

"Do you want to know the truth, Carrie? I think you can do anything you put your mind to."

"That's kind of you to say."

"It's not kindness. It's the truth. The girls somehow sensed it before I did. That's why they reached out to you the first time you met. They knew there was something inside you, something *gut*, that could lessen their pain."

"You're giving me too much credit."

"Maybe I am, but I suspect that most of the time, you don't get enough." He slid his arm around her shoulders and tilted her head toward his.

She leaned her cheek against his shirt and gazed up at the stars. There was nowhere she wanted to be and no one else she wanted to be with. The real world would return with Gerald glaring at them, but she was going to enjoy this *wunderbaar* moment now. She wasn't sure if it ever would return again.

Chapter Eleven

After swinging the saddle he'd been using onto its saddle rack, Daryn slapped dust off his jeans. He walked away from the tack room, whistling. Monty's rehabilitation was proceeding well. The horse still hadn't been ridden, but today was the first time since he'd arrived at Agua Estrella Ranch that he'd worn a saddle. He'd accepted it with the quiet aplomb he always exhibited. Walking the horse around the paddock had been a pleasure because Monty liked being with people, which amazed Daryn after the animal had been ill-treated.

"How's Monty?" came Carlos Marquez's booming voice as Daryn walked into the warm spring sunshine.

His boss was a man made of muscles that came from hard work. He was as tall as Daryn, and his hair was as ebony as his Stetson. He was a striking fellow. Not because of his jeans and cotton shirt that showed the sweat and dirt left from tending the many animals on the ranch, but because of his large black mustache that ended in waxed curls on his cheeks. He looked like he'd stepped from one of the Westerns Daryn had devoured as a kid when he'd dreamed of riding the range.

But Carlos was a man of his time, focused on his ranch and its occupants, four-legged and two-legged. His generosity in allowing Daryn to move his three nieces into the cabin that had been built as a guesthouse was as much a part of him as the scuffed boots he wore.

"Monty is improving every day," Daryn said after greeting his boss.

"Thanks to you."

"Thanks to *Doktor* Lynny. She gave him a second chance, and you're going to end up with a *gut* horse."

"Good to hear. By the way, if your ears were burning earlier, it's because I was talking about you with someone you know." Not giving Daryn a chance to decide if he wanted to ask whom Carlos was talking about, his boss went on, "Neil Malone stopped by on his way to Santa Fe."

Daryn stiffened. How had his former boss in Wyoming, the man who'd fired him before finding him a job at the Agua Estrella Ranch, dropped in to see Carlos, and Daryn was hearing about it only now? Usually news of visitors raced through the property faster than lightning could cut across the sky.

"How's he doing?" he forced himself to ask.

"It was a tough winter up there, and he lost a few head. He wanted me to pass along a message to you."

"He did?"

"Said he thought you'd want to know that Mindi had confessed."

Daryn waited for the pulse of excitement his former boss's daughter's name used to create in him. Nothing. Then he wondered about the relief he'd expected to feel when he was vindicated at long last for a crime he hadn't committed. Nothing. It was as if Carlos was talking about something that had happened to someone else.

Daryn had come to Lost River with his tail between his legs after being accused of something he hadn't known was going on until the police arrived to arrest him. He'd spent hours imagining how he'd feel when his name was cleared.

Now…nothing.

No relief. No sense of exoneration. No pleasure in knowing what Mindi faced as she admitted to her mistakes.

Somehow, he'd loosened the burden of that part of his past, letting it fly away like a no-longer-wanted balloon. He couldn't say when it had happened because he'd been too busy making a home for three *kinder* who didn't care about his past.

"It must have been horrible for you to be accused of a crime you didn't commit." Carlos sat on one of the steps to his house and motioned for Daryn to join him. When Daryn hesitated, the older man said, "You don't have to protect her any longer."

"I don't know if I was trying to protect her. I knew I hadn't been behind the wheel of that car, and I wanted to believe she hadn't, either." Dropping to sit, he locked his fingers together between his knees.

"Even when you were told you could spend years behind bars for stealing a car found to have three different types of illegal drugs hidden under the back seat and an open liquor bottle?"

"They gave me a blood test, and that proved I didn't have alcohol or drugs in my system." He stared at the mountains to the north. Beyond the passes and the highest peaks were the plains of Wyoming, which had been his home for nearly a year. "However, my fingerprints were on the car. None of the cops accepted my assertion I hadn't done anything other than clean the car earlier that day."

"Why? Didn't they ask to see what you'd used to clean it?"

He nodded. "They did, but when I went to get the buckets

and sponges, they were gone. That convinced them I was lying. When I said I hadn't had any idea it wasn't Mindi's car, the cops said I was stupid or guilty and probably both."

"You weren't guilty. I know you well enough to know that." Carlos grinned. "As far as being stupid…"

"You don't have to rub it in, but I considered her a *gut* friend. I didn't think she'd let me go to jail." He shook his head. "That *was* stupid. She didn't lift a finger to help me."

"Though Malone did. He told me he went to bat for you because he knew you were a man of integrity. His word carried a lot of weight with the district attorney. That's when he contacted me and asked if I could use a hard-working cowboy who had a way with horses."

"*Danki*, Carlos, for telling me."

"Malone was anxious you knew." The older man brushed his fingers against his lush mustache. "He's a good man, and allowing you to be blamed for something you didn't do has been weighing on him. He wanted to believe his daughter had nothing to do with the accident. He's her *daed*, and he sees her through love's eyes."

"I don't fault him." He sighed. "I wish I could let him know that, but we haven't spoken since before I left Wyoming."

"Write and tell him."

"I don't know what I'd write."

"Tell him you don't blame him for what happened." He slapped Daryn on the back, then stood. "It's a place to start, Daryn." Taking a single step, he paused and pulled an envelope from his pocket. "This came for you by registered mail. I signed for it."

Daryn took it and looked at the return address. It was the Realtor in Missouri. He came to his feet and stuffed it in his pocket when he saw a black buggy bouncing along the uneven road into the ranch.

Was it that late already? If Carrie was bringing the girls home from the Lehman farm, it meant he should have been on his way to assist Kolton and Perry with cutting more calves from the herd. The past was getting in his way again.

As he watched Carrie help the girls from the buggy and put Rae-Rae on her hip, he called, "How are you doing today?"

Carrie spun to face him. Surprise rounded her eyes and mouth before she said, "I thought you'd be on your way to help Kolton."

"I'm on my way, but do you have minute?"

"Once I get the girls inside for quiet time."

It took less than five minutes for her to settle the younger two in the bedroom for their naps and Ella with a coloring book and crayons at the table. Knowing how the youngsters liked to eavesdrop, he led Carrie outside and across the yard to Carlos's house. He sat on the steps where he had before and said nothing until she was perched next to him.

Seeing the shadows in her eyes, he wished he could toss aside everything he had to talk to her about. He would have preferred to pull her into his arms and kiss her until her eyes glowed with the joy that suffused him each time he saw her.

That couldn't be because he needed to get to work on the Lehman farm. Kolton was depending on him, and Perry, though enthusiastic, wasn't experienced enough with the bison to be a lot of help.

He pulled the envelope from his pocket. "This just arrived."

"It looks important."

"It's from the Realtor handling the sale of my brother-in-law's farm."

Her gaze rose from the envelope to his eyes. A myriad of emotions fled across her face before she asked, "What does it say?"

Ripping open the envelope, he removed several sheets of paper with small and dense writing on them. "It's an offer to purchase the farm for…" He gave a low whistle. "That's a lot more than I guessed a property with sixty acres and what Hope described as a tumbledown barn and a rickety house that might as well have been held together with string and bubble gum would be worth."

"You're going to accept it on behalf of your nieces, ain't so?"

"I can't imagine a better offer will *komm* along." He folded the pages and put them in the torn envelope. Shifting so he could face her, he asked, "How do I tell them their last connection to Missouri will be gone?"

"Why tell them anything now?"

"It's their home."

"It *was* their home." She got up and clasped her hands in front of her as she did when she was unsettled. "Daryn, they're so young. Anything you tell them will be gibberish. They don't understand about buying and selling a farm. The only thing they know about money is that a handful of change gets them candy."

He stared at the envelope. "You're right. I've been silly to worry about it."

"Nobody is suggesting you're silly to worry, but you've got to see it from their point of view."

Standing, he said, "That's not all I heard today." Before he could change his mind, he told her what Carlos had said.

Carrie listened without questions. That was so unlike her that he had to wonder if she was disgusted by what she was hearing. Did she think he'd been a *dummkopf* to get involved with self-absorbed Mindi? She had to wonder—as he did now—how he could have failed from the second he met his former boss's daughter to know that Mindi was trouble.

"I've never heard of such a thing!" Disgust dripped from each word, and he wondered how he'd win her respect back. Then he realized her repulsion wasn't aimed at him. "How could she lie like that when you'd been nice and washed the car for her when you must have had plenty of other work to do?"

"*Danki* for believing me," he said.

"Why shouldn't I believe you? You haven't lied to me."

You have no idea how many times I've lied to you, he almost replied. So many times he'd wanted to take her hand and draw her near, tilting her mouth beneath his.

They stood so close. If he slid his arm around her slender waist, would she pull away or edge toward him? Before he could go beyond that thought, her next words slammed him into reality.

"I'm sorry, Daryn, but I can't watch the girls—"

"I understand," he said, interrupting, though he didn't. Moments ago, she'd accepted his explanation of what had happened in Wyoming and she'd given him excellent advice to help his nieces. "I understand, as well, why you'd prefer not to watch the girls any longer."

Her brow furrowed. "What are you talking about?"

"You said you couldn't watch the girls—"

"Tomorrow! I never meant that I couldn't watch them otherwise." She smiled as she shook her head. "When are you going to stop seeing the worst in everything someone says or does? I know you've been betrayed, but that was someone who isn't in your life any longer."

How could he explain that his negative reactions had been

honed over the past six or seven years into an instinct? Not only an instinct but a way to protect himself from being hurt.

She doesn't want to hurt you. Was that his conscience or his heart chiding him?

"I've got an appointment tomorrow." She hesitated, then blurted, "An appointment to which I can't take the girls. I'm sorry. It came up at the last minute, and the only time available was at two. Ruthie said she can watch the girls, so I was thinking that…" She shook her head in a silent rejection of whatever she was thinking. "Never mind."

Before *gut* sense could halt him, he asked, "Never mind what?"

"I was going to ask if you'd go to the appointment with me."

"You want me to go? Why?"

"Because I want to make sure I don't miss a single word that's said. I'm worried I'll get so hung up on one thing I won't hear the next thing."

Every word she spoke confused him further. Pushing aside his other questions, he asked the one he should have right from the beginning, "Who are you meeting?"

"I have an appointment tomorrow in Lost River with Rickie Austen."

"Who's he?"

"*She* is a private investigator."

"You've got an appointment with a private detective?"

She sat on the steps again and looked up at him. It seemed odd, because he'd become accustomed to having her eyes on the same level as his. "*Ja.* I know you've been curious why I bought Greenie Gal when I already had a job as a waitress and was helping so much at home."

"I figured you'd tell me when the time was right."

"Or when the time was wrong, as it is now." She gave

him a weak smile and waved aside her words as if they didn't mean much, though he could tell they meant everything to her.

When her gaze slid away from his, he knew he had to keep the conversation going. He didn't want her to withdraw behind her cheerful facade.

"Why are you talking to a private detective?"

"To get help finding my sister. That's why I got Greenie Gal. I've been saving some of the money I'm making to hire a detective."

He frowned. "What are you going to do if you find your sister?"

"Beg Bethany to return."

"If she refuses?"

Tears flooded her eyes. "I don't know, Daryn, but I'll deal with that problem if it arises. Anticipating trouble before it arrives isn't wise. Trouble finds us soon enough as it is, ain't so?"

He flinched, then hoped she hadn't noticed. For once, her discerning gaze was turned inward, and she must have missed how he winced when she spoke what he knew was an inescapable truth.

Trouble always found him.

Had she ever had such a tough time keeping her smile in place? Carrie was sure the answer was no. As she sat in the small waiting room of an office over one of the shops in the center of Lost River, she ignored the out-of-date magazines on the side table and the television that was tuned to the Weather Channel. She pressed her hands over her abdomen and prayed she wouldn't be sick on the colorless carpet.

Daryn sat on the other chair in the room, which was on the far side of the door that opened into the hallway. He was pretending to watch the weather, but she caught his gaze slip toward her over and over. She wanted to tell him how glad she was that he was there, but she was leery of opening her mouth when her stomach roiled like a boiling pot.

The inner door opened, and a short middle-aged woman stepped out. "Carrie Detweiler?"

She jumped to her feet, then feared the contents of her stomach would explode. Taking a steadying breath, she said, "Here I am."

"Won't you come in?" She frowned when Daryn stood. "Are you together? I thought the appointment was just with you, Ms. Detweiler."

Carrie hoped she wouldn't humiliate herself, but managed to say, "I asked Daryn to join us."

The dark-haired woman whose hair was pulled back in a bun as severe as a plain woman's took her piercing gaze off Carrie and looked at him. "And you are?"

"Daryn Yutzy," he said with a serenity she wished she could emulate.

"That doesn't explain *who* you are."

"I'm a member of the same church community Carrie belongs to."

The woman evaluated them, then stepped aside to let them into her office.

Carrie hurried in before her feet could take her in the opposite direction. Glad that Daryn stood right behind her, she glanced around the space. It was more modern than the antechamber. A glass-topped table in front of the room's tall window held a computer monitor with a cell phone set next to it. The desk in the center of the room was topped by a calendar and a notepad with a trio of pens in three different colors.

"I am Rickie Austen," the woman said as she took the

chair behind the desk. She didn't add anything else until Carrie sat in the chair facing her. She didn't offer Daryn a seat, so he moved toward the glass table.

Carrie wanted to flash him a grateful grin because he was in the one spot where she could see him and Rickie at the same time. She folded her hands in her lap and gave quick answers to questions about her address and why she was seeking help while Rickie made notes on her pad.

"Missing person?" Rickie jotted something on the pad, then looked up. "To find a missing person, my standard charge is one hundred dollars per hour plus expenses."

A hundred dollars per hour? Carrie had guessed it would be less than half that, and her meager savings looked anemic. Until she had the start-up costs of her food trailer repaid, she was making less than two cents profit on each item she sold from Taters and Tales. She almost groaned when she realized she would need to sell more than five thousand burgers or packets of fries to earn enough to pay for a single hour of Rickie Austen's time.

"How long do you think you'll need to find Carrie's sister?" asked Daryn.

She thanked God she'd invited him to join her at this meeting. He'd asked the question she couldn't get her mouth to form as she faced the enormity of paying for the detective's assistance. She'd spent so much time planning for this meeting, and she was useless as she confronted the reality of what she was embarking upon.

"Finding her shouldn't take long. I have access to many databases on the state and federal levels." Rickie faltered, losing her cool poise for the first time. "Do you know what databases are?"

"*Ja*," Carrie said, straightening. This was her quest, and she couldn't stop before it had begun. "Some of our businesses make use of them. I've got a rudimentary one set up for my food business."

"I didn't know you people used computers."

"For business, we can if it's deemed necessary." She didn't explain how she'd waited for the bishop to grant his permission to activate the program that allowed her to track events where her trailer could participate as well as establishing reorder points for her supplies and trends for food her customers preferred.

"Good. That will make things easier for you to understand." Rickie folded her arms on the desk and leaned forward. "The first stumbling block I see is that your sister is Amish."

"She may not be living a plain life."

"But will she have a driver's license or a credit card or a phone in her name?" She looked at the notes she'd been taking. "Did you mention if she's married or not?"

"I don't know if she is."

"The man she left with—"

"I don't know his name or if the man I saw her talking to several times here in town is the man she left with."

Daryn added, "Or if she left with him." When Carrie gasped as Rickie's eyes narrowed, he hurried to add, "You said once, Carrie, that you weren't sure if she went with someone else or not."

"I meant I didn't know if someone in the community helped her. I never thought…" Why hadn't she given more thought to the idea that Bethany had jumped the fence for a reason other than love? How many times in the past two years had she wondered, as her family's protective arms tightened around her until she felt strangled, if Bethany had felt the same before she vanished?

By the time the appointment was over, Carrie left feeling

like a sheet going through the wringer and a hundred-and-fifty dollars poorer. She had written the check for everything she had in the bank except for the money she'd set aside for the supplies she'd need for the art festival in Dashtown next weekend. The private detective assured her that a clue to where Bethany was might be uncovered more quickly than ninety minutes.

Carrie prayed Rickie would be right. If Taters and Tales did a bang-up business in Dashtown, she would have enough profit to pay for another half hour.

Daryn opened the door at the bottom of the stairs and held it while she stepped onto the sun-washed street. A breeze was blowing from the west, sending small spirals of dust along the wide road that was a straight line through the center of Lost River.

Neither spoke until they were in the buggy that had been left by a hitching pole farther along the street. When Daryn turned it south toward the ranch, Carrie said, "This could be more difficult than I imagined if she can't find a database with Bethany's name in it right away."

"She'll be doing the heavy lifting. You need to be ready with any information that will make her job easier."

"I don't have anything else."

"What about your sister's favorite foods?"

"How will that help?"

"You said she loves to bake as much as you like to cook." He edged the buggy around a car that was making a left turn as they drove toward the distant mountains to the east. In the bright sunlight, the mountains were pale gray lumps on the horizon. "If she's on her own, or if she needs money, wouldn't she use her skills?"

"You mean I should have Rickie start checking bakeries?"

"*Ja.*"

"But there must be dozens in the valley, and I don't know if she stayed in the San Luis Valley or went beyond it."

"I didn't say it would be easy, but it's a place to start."

"If it's a dead end?"

"What do you say? There's a solution for every dilemma."

She rolled her eyes. "Please don't throw my words in my face. Don't you know it's easier to give advice than to take it?"

"But it was *gut* advice, and I know you. Not only do you have a plan A—hiring Rickie—but you've got a plan B and a plan C and more plans to the end of the alphabet."

"I've had two years to think about this."

He pushed the toggle to turn on the signal lights for a right turn. "Okay, so do you think checking bakeries would be a smart place to begin?"

"It's as *gut* a place as any."

"But?"

She closed her eyes, but she couldn't banish the thought that had been plaguing her from the moment she opened the door to Rickie's office. At last, she gave it voice. "What if Bethany doesn't want to be found?"

Chapter Twelve

The crowds filled the few streets of the former mining town of Dashtown, which had rebranded itself as an arts community while still celebrating its mining heritage. Sheer walls of stone rose straight up from the small creek that ran along one side of the village. In the center of town, situated in the San Juan Mountains to the west of Lost River, its row of late Victorian shops had been painted in a rainbow of colors. Houses were built up the side of one slope, but the cliffs at the far end narrowed until there was barely enough room for the stream and a road to go between them.

Daryn was amazed as he pushed the stroller along the sidewalk and looked around the bustling main street. He'd become accustomed to living where there were miles of land between him and the horizon in every direction. Here he felt as if the mountainsides were about to pounce on the people and buildings.

Only to the south did the space open up. There the railroad had been built to bring ore from Dashtown, its tracks following the stream that wandered along gravel banks. In that direction, the town had been built around a park that once had been part of a decommissioned railroad depot. Now it held the town's historical museum. A bandstand at one end of the park blared with the cacophony of a quartet doing sound checks with equipment that didn't want to cooperate.

Greenie Gal was parked in the middle of a line of trucks and other trailers. A couple were offering burgers and fries, but hers was the only one with poutine on the menu. From where he stood in front of a shop that sold T-shirts and ice cream, he could see a crowd gathering to peruse her menu.

He crossed the street with his nieces in tow, watching for cars though the traffic had been stopped for the town's Last Blast Days. From reading the brochure someone had passed to him as he walked around the tents where people could make art in the middle of the street, he knew the festival had been named for the mine which had brought thousands of miners to Dashtown in hopes of striking it rich. The Last Blast Mine, which wasn't visible from Main Street, had been found late one afternoon by the man who'd given his name to the town. Pictures of Aloysius Dash were hanging from every light pole, his face nearly lost behind his bushy sideburns.

"Go on pony rides?" Kayla asked.

"Rides!" Rae-Rae repeated.

"Cotton candy?"

"Candy!"

"Ice cream. Me want ice cream!"

"Cream. Yum."

The two younger girls didn't miss a thing for sale along the street, and they wanted him to see each item too. They kept up the singsong rhythm, but Ella was silent. Her eyes were flicking from side to side. More than once, he'd thought she was about to say something, but each time her teeth gripped her lower lip so she couldn't speak.

How he'd hoped she would enjoy the day! After signing the papers to sell the Byler farm, he'd been feeling guilty that he'd done it without telling his nieces. He knew Carrie had been right. Informing them would add to their sorrow, and they wouldn't have understood why he'd made the decision he had. Once the property closed, the money would be put in trust for the girls, so they would have a *gut* start on their adult lives. He planned to talk to the bishop and get Jerek's advice on how to invest the funds so they would grow as the girls did.

"Howdy! Howdy! Howdy!" Carrie's joy-filled voice sent his thoughts fleeing. Waving to them from where her trailer was set between one selling geodes and another offering an assortment of hard candy sticks, she said, "I was hoping you'd stop by Taters and Tales."

"Books?" asked Ella, surprising her sisters as much as him.

"I've got special books at home for you." She winked at the *kinder*. "I thought you'd like something to eat. Who wants poutine?"

The girls called, "Me!"

Carrie pointed toward her hand-lettered menu. "Here are your poutine choices today."

"Can't read," lamented Kayla.

"Shall I read it for you?" Daryn asked, glad for any excuse to step closer to Carrie. "The top one is Three Little Pigs Poutine."

"That one has bacon bits," Carrie explained to his nieces, "and sausage and ham with cheese on the fries."

He ran his finger down the menu. "The Unmannerly Tiger Poutine. Is that named after a story, too?"

"*Ja.* 'The Unmannerly Tiger' is a Korean fairy tale about a tiger who wasn't grateful when his life was saved and ended up paying the price. Sort of a morality tale, like one from *Aesop's Fables*. The poutine has strips of cheese and soy sauce to recreate a tiger's stripes as well as kimchee for a spicy kick."

"And Alice's Wonderland Poutine?"

"Mushrooms and eggs on cheese and fries, of course." She smiled. "The mushroom is from the first book and the egg is for Humpty Dumpty in *Through the Looking Glass.* It's my vegetarian choice."

"No tea party to go with it?"

She chuckled. "I've been thinking that if I decide to start a catering company, I could offer a Mad Hatter's tea to go with the Wonderland Poutine."

"You're going to have to have March Rarebit with it, ain't so?"

Her eyes flashed with delight, and he wondered if his were doing the same. Making her happy seemed as delicious an idea as eating her poutine. "What a fabulous idea, even though it was a March hare!"

"Close enough, ain't so?"

"*Ja.* I need to devise something with a dormouse and a little girl and a hat."

"You will." He peered at the menu. "What? You don't have plain old poutine?"

"Right here. Annie's Green Island Poutine."

He nodded. "For *Anne of Green Gables.* You can't get much more Prince Edward Island than that."

After repeating the choices to the girls, he gave them a minute to discuss which they wanted. He took the time to ask, "Have you heard from Rickie?"

She paused as she was opening the door to the trailer. Glancing in both directions, she must have been looking for her family. She hadn't said, but he knew she didn't want them to know she'd contacted a private detective. It amazed him how he could read her true feelings when she wore her happy mask.

"Your family is at the far end of the street," he said. "I saw your *daed* talking with a man who makes art from old farm equipment. I could tell Gerald and Perry were itching to slip away."

"Rickie doesn't think Bethany is in the San Luis Valley, but she can check anywhere in the United States easily."

"What if Bethany went to Canada or somewhere else?"

Carrie shrugged. "Do you know that it was two years ago tonight Bethany left?"

"No, I didn't." He wasn't sure what to say.

She saved him from replying when she climbed into the trailer and wrote the choices the girls had made. Her professional cheerfulness returned as she took other orders as well and began cooking. It was as easy to admire her skill in preparing the food as it was to delight in her pretty face and welcoming chatter.

She handed him the containers holding one order of Three Little Pigs Poutine and two orders of The Unmannerly Tiger Poutine. She asked about kimchi before putting it on the servings. As one was for him, he had her add the spicy cabbage and peppers to his plate.

Finding a place where they could sit and eat, Daryn kept an eye on the trailer where Carrie was in her element. He watched as each *kind* went away with a book. Kids who didn't order anything were offered a book, too. Around him, youngsters were reading, oblivious to everything else. Her dream of instilling her love of reading in others was coming true.

Daryn couldn't loiter in the park while Carrie was hard at work. He took his nieces to visit the displays and shops. Though they'd had their fill of poutine, they pointed out every sweet. He waited an hour before he allowed them each to pick something. After that, he made sure neither the stroller nor the girls got close to the art on display. He didn't want sticky fingerprints on a canvas or sculpture.

As the sun set and the evening twilight thickened, the vendors began to close up so everyone attending could participate in painting a mural on the side of one of the old buildings. Bright lights glared off the whitewashed surface where people were gathering. He guessed his nieces would be too small to join in, so he led them to where Carrie was shutting down her trailer. She welcomed his nieces with enthusiasm and chocolate chip cookies.

"One of the other food truck people dropped them off in exchange for poutine," she said as she handed each girl a cookie, then offered him one. "From what I've heard, these are the best cookies available today."

"Are you set? Would you like a break?" he asked after taking a bite of the scrumptious cookie.

She smiled. "You look as if you could use one yourself."

"I've been busy with keeping little hands away from valuable art." So she didn't think he was complaining when he hadn't done much more than walk around town while she worked in her food trailer, he added, "It's not hard to distract them with food."

"*Ach*, girls after my own heart." Squatting, she tapped each of his nieces on the nose. They giggled. She looked up at him. "How about a walk?"

"The five of us?"

"I was thinking the girls would enjoy being spoiled by my parents. *Daed* and *Mamm* keep asking when they'll visit the farm again." She stood. "I'd like to look around town, but only if we don't talk about the past."

"That sounds like the best idea I've heard in the longest time."

When she smiled at him, he wondered if his feet had left the pavement. He seemed to be floating on air, standing a little bit taller than he had in years.

Mamm and *Daed* agreed to watch Daryn's nieces while he gave Carrie a tour of the small town before it got too dark. They mentioned Gerald had been heading to the fudge shop, and Perry had found guys his age and planned to wander up to see what was left of the mine. *Mamm* remarked on the last with a bit of concern, and Carrie had been about to ask if she wanted them to check on the teens. However, a glance in the direction of the narrowing cliffs showed the silhouettes of four tall boys walking toward town, so *Mamm* urged her and Daryn to go and have fun. Before the two of them were out of earshot, Kayla was already babbling about what she'd eaten and seen.

"They'll have a *gut* time," Carrie assured him when she saw furrows in his forehead.

"The girls or your parents?"

She laughed as she matched her steps to his. The sidewalks emptied when visitors joined the painters in the middle of town. "Both. Gerald has been getting hints my parents would love to be *grossmammi* and *grossdawdi*."

"That's what he gets for being the oldest. I remember when Hope lamented that our parents needed to be more patient about her giving them *kins-kinder.* Oops! We agreed we wouldn't talk about the past."

Taking his hand, she cradled it between hers as she stopped and faced him. The voices around them faded while they stood on the sidewalk like a pair of islands in the middle of the river of people. "It's not possible to escape it. It's part of us like each breath we take."

"True, but that doesn't mean we have to invite it to join us with every breath we take."

"I've got to remember that," she whispered, looking at their hands as he laced their fingers together. "You can be wise sometimes."

"And far from wise most of the time." Holding her hand, he continued with her along the sidewalk toward the creek that was tumbling from a cleft where the cliffs had been broken apart sometime in the ancient past. Its eager song as it sought flatter ground was as sweet as the last songs of the day that birds were trilling in the nearby trees. "Maybe that's why I'm considering training to become a volunteer firefighter in Lost River. Kolton has been after me to give it a try."

"He loves that work, ain't so?"

"*Ja*, and he's the first to admit it's tough work. Tough and dangerous."

She gave a gentle shiver. "I've heard how he's rushed into more than one burning building to save a person or animals."

"He's said he'd have to think twice now that he has kids and a wife."

"Do you think he'd stand back and let someone else go in?"

Daryn shook his head as they paused by a small dam that created a pond at the town's edge. Shadows from the tall cliffs darkened the water. "Not likely. He's not that kind of man."

"You're not, either. You'd have to keep that in mind if you sign up. You must be ready to let someone else take the risk if that's what's best for fighting a fire."

He halted as a gust sent cottonwood fuzz swirling

through the air like a spring snowstorm. It curled around their feet before floating along the road. "Is that your way of reminding me that I'm responsible for three little girls?"

"You said having a family has given Kolton second thoughts about rushing into a fire. I figured that meant you'd had second thoughts, too."

"Second and third and fourth about things as simple as who would watch the girls if I'm called to a fire. They're too young for me to leave them alone."

"*Doktor* Lynny—"

"Is on call."

She patted his hand that she held as they turned toward town, walking through the clumps of cottonwood seeds that clung to the edges of the road. "Don't forget you've got us to help. You just need to ask."

"Asking isn't easy for me."

"It's not easy for anyone, but God didn't put us here to live our lives without others around us."

"Now who is sounding wise?"

Carrie stared in amazement. "You're smiling!"

"I am?"

Knowing she was being bold, she ran her finger across his lips. "See? They're tilting up. Could it be that you're happy, Daryn Yutzy? Happy enough so you can't hide it?"

"*Ja*," he whispered with abrupt intensity. "I am happy, but I'll be happier when I..." He grasped her by the shoulders and pulled her to him so quickly that her *kapp* bounced on her head.

Before she could react, his mouth found hers. She froze in shock before melting against him as her arms slipped around his shoulders. His wind-roughened cheek brushed her face. When his lips moved to caress her eyelids and forehead, she steered his mouth back to hers.

"Carrie," he murmured against her lips.

Whatever else he might have intended to say went unsaid as shouts came from the center of town. She looked past him to see people pointing toward the buildings closest to the park.

"What's going on?" he asked.

Carrie grabbed his hand and began to run toward the crowd. "I don't know, but let's find out."

The shouts grew louder as they reached the others. She scanned the crowd for her family. There they were! Her parents were off to one side, not far from her food trailer. It and several other vendors' vehicles were surrounded by people.

"Let's get to *Mamm* and *Daed*." She didn't release his hand while she found her way through the throng. Not only did she want to avoid losing him in the crowd, but she couldn't bear being so far from him after they'd been so close. "They'll know what has happened."

"The girls?" Anxiety stripped every other emotion from his voice.

"With my folks." She stood on tiptoe, which allowed her to see over the top of most people's heads. "Gerald is headed this way. Where's Perry?"

"Over there."

She looked where he was pointing, and horror swept the joy from her. Perry stood in the light from the street lamps in the middle of the street with a cop on either side of him.

Trouble.

Daryn recognized the signs from experience. Bad experience. He recognized Carrie's expression. Dismay mixed with disbelief and denial. He'd seen that same expression on his brother's face when Daryn had been in trouble…again.

"Wait with your family," he said beneath the rumbles of

conversation from the people around them, speculating on what was going on.

"I should—"

"Let me do this. I know what I'm doing."

Her eyes searched his, seeking confirmation for his words. She must have found it because she nodded and squeezed his arm. "I'll go and keep the girls calm."

He wished they could return to their stroll through town. Then, for a few *wunderbaar* minutes, his only concern had been when he'd kiss her and how she'd react. He wanted to wrap those memories around him like a turtle in its shell to banish the rest of the world.

Daryn pushed his way through the crowd that was trying to get a better look at what was happening in the middle of the street. As he emerged from the wall of people, he saw three other teens. Each had a uniformed officer holding his arm. Those boys were surrounded by yelling people. When the kids hung their heads, he knew they were the targets of the angry voices.

He turned to where Perry stood with two cops. Surprised the small town had so many police officers, Daryn wondered if some were auxiliaries who worked special events in Dashtown. Those officers might react differently than regular cops, so he should be prepared. Though he wondered how he could prepare himself. He'd always been the one standing with the cop, not the one trying to find out what was going on.

As he approached, the shorter of the two officers, a man in his forties, looked him up and down, taking note of his plain clothing. In an arrogant tone, he asked, "Is this kid part of your family?"

"No, but he works for me." That was stretching the truth

a bit, but Carlos and Kolton had had him supervise Perry on multiple occasions.

"So he has a job?"

"Two. He works with horses at the Agua Estrella Ranch in Lost River, and he also works with bison at a nearby farm."

That brought a surprised expression from the other officer who'd been silent while he tapped notes into his phone. He was taller, also in his mid-forties. Daryn guessed he was a full-time cop by his unruffled demeanor. *Gut!* He preferred to deal with someone who didn't have anything to prove.

"And you are?" asked the taller officer.

"Daryn Yutzy. I live on the Agua Estrella Ranch."

"How long have you known this boy?"

Perry bristled at being called a boy, but a quick glance from Carrie's *daed* who appeared from the crowd kept him silent.

"About a month and a half," Daryn replied.

The policeman made a note on his tablet. "Not long."

"Long enough to know he's a hard worker and does what he's told."

"Usually?" A smile pulled at the officer's mouth, and Daryn guessed he was a *daed* of a teen himself or had had plenty of run-ins with them.

"Usually." He wasn't going to reveal his arguments with Perry about getting work done on time. "What's the problem?"

"He and three local lads were caught drawing graffiti on the town museum and other things in the park."

"In the park?" He looked toward where Carrie's shuttered Greenie Gal waited for its tow to Lost River. From where he stood, he could see red paint splashed across the old trailer.

His brows lowered as he turned to the teen. "You vandalized your cousin's trailer?"

"I didn't do it!" Perry's defiance hadn't dimmed a bit. "You can't prove anything, Daryn Yutzy."

"I don't have to prove anything. I'm not the one accused of a crime." Looking at the policeman, Daryn knew his motion would irk the teen. *Gut!* The boy needed to start realizing he didn't know everything. If he'd been involved with the vandalism, he had to face up to the consequences.

"Officer...?"

"Charlie Baylor," the man supplied.

Carrie's *daed* spoke for the first time. "I'm Malachi Detweiler. Officer Baylor, may we talk to you somewhere more private?"

"Are you his father?"

"He's my nephew, but I'm his guardian along with my wife." He didn't look in Perry's direction.

Officer Baylor nodded and gestured to the T-shirt shop behind him. "There's a place where we can talk in there. The rest of you stay here." His eyes narrowed as he imprisoned Perry in his gaze. "Don't even think about trying to slip away."

The teen muttered something and shoved his glasses up his nose, but didn't move as the other cop stepped closer to him. As Malachi and Officer Baylor climbed up on the wood porch and disappeared into the shop, Carrie and her *mamm* approached with Daryn's nieces. Carrie glanced in his direction, but went to ask Perry if he was okay. He didn't answer and refused to return Alberta's embrace.

Daryn turned away before he shouted that Perry should recognize how blessed he was to have his family show they cared for him, no matter what he'd done. But the teen was making the same stupid show of contempt and bravado Daryn had at his age.

Perry needed to accept his family would be right at his side…if he allowed them to. When Daryn had first done much the same type of prank as Perry was accused of, his brother had been more than willing to listen to his side of the story and to help him deal with the consequences.

Daryn had been as ungrateful for the support as Perry was now. Then Daryn had left, never telling his brother how much he respected Mark's persistence in trying to convince Daryn he wasn't a bad kid. He owed his brother an apology. A big one.

It was five hours later before Carrie and her family were given permission to leave Dashtown with her cousin. Paige had arrived with her truck before full dark to take the vandalized food trailer to the Detweiler farm. Not wanting to satisfy her friend's curiosity when she had so many questions of her own, Carrie had remained in the small former mining town with her family.

Shortly before midnight, Perry was released into the custody of her parents. She wanted to grab him and try to shake sense into his thick head. Instead of grumbling and saying things under his breath she guessed she didn't want to hear, he should have been telling *Daed* how much he appreciated his help.

Perry didn't seem to hold a grudge against Gerald. Her cousin must not have heard how her older brother suggested they leave Perry in the local jail until he learned a lesson. If she'd reminded Gerald of his phone calls and texts to show him that their cousin wasn't the only one challenging the rules, that would have started an argument. *Mamm* displayed the signs of an oncoming headache, and getting her home so she could rest was paramount.

The little girls had fallen asleep on a blanket in the police station while the necessary questions were asked and paperwork completed. The local teens left with their parents a half hour before Perry was allowed to go. She hadn't been sure what the cops were trying to check.

"I don't want to believe he's involved, Daryn," she'd whispered as they waited in the far corner of the police station's open room.

"But?"

"I know he must be. I saw him with the other boys earlier in the afternoon. My trailer offers a great view of the whole park, and I happened to see them near the restrooms at one end of the park. At the time, I was pleased he'd found friends. I didn't give any thought to the idea that they might not be proper friends."

"How were you to know?" He'd shoved his hands into his pockets. "I was supposed to be helping with him. You've done so much for the girls, and I've fallen down on the job."

"You've done what you could. We each own our mistakes."

"I've learned that."

Putting her hand on his arm, she was relieved when he curled his fingers around hers. Touching him gave her the strength to ask, "What will happen?"

"If Colorado is anything like Wyoming, he'll have to go to court and tell his side of the story to a judge."

"Like you did?"

"*Ja.*" His mouth had become a straight line. "I hope he'll be believed."

"You weren't?"

"No."

She waited for him to add more, but he was silent. What thoughts were going through his head as his mind replayed the scenes that tormented him? She squeezed his hand, hoping the motion would say more than words could how much she appreciated having him in her life.

His words replayed in her head during the silent ride home while she sat between Gerald and Perry, who refused to acknowledge the existence of any of them. They repeated while she got ready for bed and said her prayers, asking God to reach Perry as they'd failed to. Not even her cousin's raised voice from downstairs obliterated Daryn's voice from her memory. It crawled into her dreams, chasing her.

Then another voice erupted through the night. Her *mamm*'s frantic voice shouting, "He's gone!"

Groggily getting up and pulling on a robe, Carrie headed for the stairs. She saw her parents and brother in the middle of the living room.

"Who's gone?" she asked, fighting a yawn.

It collapsed, uncompleted, when her *daed* said, "Perry. He's disappeared."

Chapter Thirteen

Carrie gripped the stair railing. Gone? Perry was gone?

"Doesn't he realize how guilty this will make him look?" she murmured.

"He's not thinking about that."

Daryn! How had Daryn gotten there so quickly?

As if she'd asked, Daryn said, "I decided to stop in and see how things were going. I thought Perry might want to talk."

"Where are the girls?"

"Asleep in the buggy." He turned to her parents. "I can guarantee you Perry isn't thinking of anything but getting away from the mess."

She came down the rest of the steps so she could see his taut face. "Is that what you did, Daryn?"

"*Ja.*" He held her gaze. "I thought if I ran far enough, it wouldn't catch up with me."

Puzzlement drew lines across her parents' brows, but she didn't stop to explain. It was Daryn's past and his story to tell. Right now, it was more important to find Perry.

"We'll need help," she said.

Mamm swayed and put her hand on the sofa. Her face was drawn with pain and fear for her nephew. "I can send

Gerald to alert Kolton. He and the other firefighters have done searches for lost hikers."

"It'll be better if we keep this low-key," Daryn replied. "We don't want to drive him to ground. Let me get help from the ranch, and I'll be back."

Daed moved toward the door. "Gerald and I will start going through the buildings here. Carrie, get dressed and bring the little girls inside. Once they're settled, join us."

She nodded, then rushed up the stairs. Going into her room, she reached for her dress and *kapp* on their pegs on her side of the bedroom. She froze when she heard a soft sound.

Was it Perry? No, that didn't make sense. He wouldn't be hiding in her room.

The rustle came again. It didn't sound like a mouse or a squirrel that had found its way into the house. It sounded like fabric. Behind her.

She turned and stared at the silhouette in the doorway. The shadows couldn't hide the truth from her. She knew the curve of that face as surely as she knew her own.

"Bethany?" Not believing her question, she groped around the bed and switched on the battery-operated lamp on the table between her bed and her sister's.

Looking back at the door, she struggled to breathe. It *was* her sister. The scenarios she'd imagined had revolved around her and her sister running to each other and hugging. That fantasy fell away as she stared at her motionless sister's familiar face.

But it was different.

Bethany's usual smile was missing, and deep half circles of gray arced beneath her green eyes. Lines were scored into her forehead as if she'd spent too much time frowning.

However, the biggest difference was the *boppli* wrapped

in a blanket. No, not a blanket. It was the bright blue and yellow quilt that *Grossmammi* had made for Carrie and Bethany when they were born, the quilt Bethany had taken the night she vanished. Now, she held it and the *boppli* close to her.

"*Gut owed*, Carrie," her twin said as if they were strangers.

Carrie ached to rush forward and take them both in her arms and hold them until the pain of the past two years was gone. She didn't. Unlike before, there was an invisible wall between them. Everything about her sister's posture warned Carrie to stay away. A sob sliced through Carrie, as pointed as a needle, but somehow she restrained it enough so she could speak.

"Do you want to sit?" She motioned toward the chair by the window.

Her gaze took in every bit of her sister. Bethany had cut her hair. It hung over her shoulders in thick blond curls. The same curls that were on the *kind*'s head, though those were dark brown and blended in with Bethany's black shirt. She wore navy pants and sneakers covered with dried mud.

Where had her twin been walking? Another question she couldn't ask when so much else needed to be explained. Starting with why her sister had returned…and whose *boppli* was she holding.

Boppli! She must get the Byler girls from the buggy before they woke up and found themselves alone. If they wandered off, they could get hurt. Drainage ditches along the side of the roads were deep enough to be a danger to small *kinder*.

Pulling on her dress and closing it, Carrie said, "I need to go outside for a minute." She stopped and stared at her twin who was crossing the room. A change, because Bethany had been like Kayla. Never walking when she could dance or skip. "Don't leave. Please."

"I won't."

Though she wanted to ask her sister to promise, she nodded and shut the door. She ran into the yard to retrieve Daryn's nieces. Lights moved along the barns, marking where *Daed* and Gerald were looking for Perry. She wanted to shout that Bethany was in the house, but something stopped her. Though her twin hadn't said anything, Carrie had sensed she didn't want to face the whole family yet.

She hurried to the buggy. The two older girls were able to walk into the house, but she carried Rae-Rae. She was about to tell them to use the couch, then realized *Mamm* was there with her eyes closed.

For a second, Carrie hesitated. Would it ease *Mamm*'s agony if she knew her other daughter had returned? Or would the shock increase her pain? First, Carrie must get the little girls settled. Then, she'd deal with the complications of Bethany's homecoming and get about a thousand questions answered.

Taking the *kinder* upstairs to her parents' room, she tucked them into the wide bed. They were so exhausted they didn't pester her for a story or a drink of water. All three were asleep as soon as their heads touched the pillows.

Carrie went to the room next door. Her fingers shook as she opened the door. What if Bethany had left? Or if this was a dream and her sister had never returned?

She breathed a soft prayer of gratitude when she saw her sister sitting by the window. It was the same chair where Bethany had spent so much of her free time reading recipes before trying them and sharing the results with her family.

Her twin's head was drooping, and Carrie rushed forward. Half asleep, Bethany pulled back, her arms tightening around the *boppli* which let out a startled cry.

"You're exhausted," Carrie said. Bethany must rest. In the

morning, when Bethany wasn't ready to drop from fatigue, maybe everything would be the way Carrie had imagined. "I've got an extra nightgown in the drawer. It'll be too long for you, but if you want to change, I can hold the *boppli*. He—she—"

"He. His name is Aidan."

Carrie bit her lower lip so she didn't ask her next question. Aidan wasn't a plain name. That could mean his *daed* hadn't been plain. Was he the *Englischer* Carrie had seen her sister talking to at the grocery store?

"He needs to be changed." Bethany stood. "I'm not going to ask you to do that."

"I can."

"I know you can, but I'm not going to ask you to do it."

"Why not?" She wasn't sure why she was pushing the issue, but every word and every motion was a reminder of how Bethany's return shouldn't have been like this. "Isn't that what a twin is supposed to do for her twin? Help her?"

"Enough, Carrie!" Bethany's voice snapped like static electricity through the room. When Aidan began to fuss, she tempered her volume. "If you want it to be a twin thing, then will you understand your twin is exhausted? Will you leave us alone so we can sleep?"

Leaving her sister alone was the last thing she wanted to do. She wanted to hug her, to sit and talk through the night as they shared what had happened to them during the past two years, to tell her sister about the glorious kisses Daryn had given her that day. She longed for them to laugh together, lament together, cheer together as they once had done.

But she'd told *Daed* she'd help him look for Perry. What would he do when he learned his other daughter was back?

"Don't say a word tonight to *Daed* and *Mamm*," Bethany said, warning Carrie that her sister could read her thoughts and emotions with ease. "I can't face them and their mixed welcome home and guilt trip for their wandering daughter tonight."

"Tomorrow?" She kept her voice low, so as not to wake the little girls on the other side of the wall.

"I'm not thinking that far ahead. I want to sleep. It's been a long trip here."

From where? Carrie's hands closed into fists as she fought her frustration.

"All right," she said, knowing *Daed* might *komm* in if she didn't join the search. "May I see your son?"

She couldn't miss her sister's reluctance as she drew back the blanket that had obscured everything but the little one's dark curls. His eyes were half closed, so she couldn't guess what color they were. The *kind*'s round cheeks were dirty as if he and Bethany hadn't had a chance to bathe in a few days. From what Carrie could see, Aidan must be close in age to Rae-Rae. That meant her sister must have been pregnant before she jumped the fence, as rumor had supposed.

"He's beautiful," she said to cover her shock. "You always said you'd have a boy first. Aidan Det—"

"His last name is Houlihan," she said without a hint of emotion. "Like mine."

"You're married?"

"Not any longer."

She gasped. "What happened?"

"Mike is dead. It's just Aidan and me."

She moved to embrace her sister, but froze when Bethany edged away.

Bethany set the *boppli* on the bed, and a stuffed toy fell from the blanket. Patches! Bethany's beloved bear.

Carrie was reaching for it before she could halt herself,

but jerked back her hand when Bethany said, "Can't you just leave us alone tonight?"

Blinking on hot tears as she closed the door behind her, Carrie slunk along the hall, too hurt by her twin's sharp tone to respond.

No, this reunion was nothing as Carrie had imagined. Instead of a dream, it was a nightmare.

Daryn wasn't surprised to see a few lights on at the Detweiler house when he pulled into the yard. He'd sent a couple of his ranch coworkers along the county road east toward the diner where Carrie worked and another pair north in the direction of Lost River. How familiar was Perry with the roads to the south?

He checked in with Malachi, but as he'd expected, there hadn't been any signs Perry was still on the farm. Carrie's *daed* looked as if he'd aged two decades in the past half hour.

Carrie came in while he was talking with her *daed*. She seemed subdued. Was it her cousin running away, or was something else on her mind? He couldn't believe she regretted the kisses they'd shared in Dashtown. He didn't. In fact, it took all his willpower *not* to tug her to him and taste those fragrant lips.

"Okay," he said, after explaining where he'd sent the men to search, "I'll alert Kolton. I want to head that way because I've thought of a couple of places where he may be."

"Take me with you," Carrie said.

His gaze swept over her face, and he nodded. Why was she looking as if every dream she'd ever had was dashed? The usual joy that shone from her eyes seemed to have been carved out of her, leaving her hollow. What had happened since he'd last seen her less than a half hour ago? He could think of one reason for her disquiet.

"The girls—" he began.

"We can talk on the way. Let's not waste more time." To Malachi, she said, "I put Daryn's nieces in your bed, *Daed. Mamm's* on the sofa. I'm sure she'd appreciate you getting her a damp cloth to cover her eyes."

Carrie was silent as they went to where his buggy waited. She said nothing while they drove onto the blacktop and headed toward the Lehman farm. When a sports car raced past them at a perilous speed, she was mute. As if, he realized with a pulse of shock, she was Ella.

As they slowed for a stop sign, he looked at her. "What's happened, Carrie? Is something wrong with one of the girls?"

"Your nieces are fine." Her voice broke as she said, "When I went up to my room to change, my sister was there."

"Bethany?" It was a stupid question. She had one sister, her twin. "She's back?"

"Up in our room with her son."

His head reeled as he listened to her outline what had happened. Tonight, when the Detweilers were facing such a mess with Perry, was the one Bethany had chosen to return. Of course she couldn't have known what was happening. Or had she learned about it somehow and seen the confusion as a way to slip into the house unnoticed by her parents?

He didn't ask that question, not wanting to add to the hurt he heard in Carrie's voice. Instead he asked, "Will she move in with her *boppli*?"

"I wish I could say *ja*, but I don't know if she's staying."

"Did she say she's planning to leave?"

"No, but she didn't say she was planning to stay." A shudder went through her voice as she asked, "If you went home, would you stay?"

He yearned to be able to say the words he knew she

wanted to hear. Words to reassure her that everything would go back to the way it'd been before Bethany left…and before she'd returned with a *boppli*. He wouldn't lie to Carrie.

"I don't know," he said. "I honestly don't know, Carrie."

She turned away. To hide her tears or her worry that Lost River was a temporary stop on her sister's journey?

"*Danki* for being honest with me," she said.

"You need to be honest with your sister. Ask her."

"As long as I don't know, I can hope."

"While you're wracked with fear." He put his hand over her clasped ones on her lap. "If Bethany is like you, there's a reason why she's here. You don't do things on a whim."

"Not even kiss you?"

He smiled, relieved it was easy. As it should have always been. He'd been the one preventing himself from embracing life.

"You're welcome to kiss me anytime you want." He turned the buggy into the farm lane leading to the Lehman farm. "Except right now while we see if Perry is here."

Daryn stepped from the buggy, Carrie a second behind him. When he started for the barns, she followed. Rain began to mist, the first rain they'd had that spring. He stopped, and she bumped into him. He held his finger to his lips, then to hers, before motioning for her to go with him.

He went to the bison calving barn, which was a simple structure. Open on one side to a smaller pasture, it was divided into two parts, so two bison could be supervised while giving birth. Kolton had designed it so the bison cows felt safe and able to protect their calves from a predator.

On quick glance, it looked empty. He switched the lights on, splashing the whole area in a dim glow as rain fell harder. Supplies were stacked on the low wall between the birthing pens, and hay had been piled in the two corners.

Daryn put a finger to his lips again and pointed at the far pen. Carrie nodded and remained where she was as he walked toward it.

"Perry, you might as well get up," he said. "I can see an obvious lump in the hay."

Daryn held his breath as he wondered if the teen would respond. If Perry refused to emerge, what would Daryn do? If he went to alert Kolton, Perry could be long gone by the time he got back. As shattered as Carrie was by her sister's return, would she be able to stop the kid from racing away?

The hay stirred, and Perry stood. The boy brushed bits of the broken stalks from his clothes and hair. Or he tried to. The pieces stuck to him as if pressed on with glue. He shifted his glasses on his nose.

"Are you okay?" asked Carrie into the silence.

Perry's head snapped up. "I didn't think you'd *komm* looking for me."

"There are a lot of people worried about you." Her voice was toneless. "When we should be focusing on other things."

Daryn saw shock on the teen's face. Perry didn't know Bethany had returned home, so he couldn't comprehend the odd sound of Carrie's voice. When the boy looked at him, Daryn shook his head. He hoped Perry would understand that questions had to wait while he gave answers.

Apparently not, because the teen asked, "How did you know I was here?"

The question was aimed at him, so Daryn answered it, "Because when I was your age and I wanted to run away, I went somewhere I could be less miserable." He arched his eyebrows. "I wasn't looking to be happy. I don't think I could have been happy then. But I remember there were times when I felt less miserable, and, for me, that was the chance to work with animals. It's the same for you, ain't so?"

"Is that how you knew to *komm* here?"

"I guessed you'd be here or at Agua Estrella Ranch. With so many people at the ranch, it would be easier for you to hide here." He leaned his shoulder against an upright post. "Look, Perry. I know what you're thinking. I've been you. You're thinking you can run away. Let me tell you. No matter how far you run, you can't run far enough to escape the problems you've left behind. Trust me. I've tried. No matter how many times I fled from my mistakes, they caught up with me. Every time."

"Is that supposed to make me feel better? It's a lousy pep talk."

Rather than respond to the boy's sarcasm, Daryn said, "Carrie, let me talk to him by myself."

She hesitated, then said, "If you think you can help him better that way, okay."

"I don't know if it'll make a difference, but I need you to trust me as you asked me to the first day you were watching the girls for me." He took her hands and held them between his. "Can you?"

"*Ja.*" She looked past him to where Perry was rolling a pebble around with the toe of his boot. "I'll wait in the buggy."

"No," he said. "Go home."

"But I want to help."

"You can. At home. Let everyone know that he's been found."

"All right."

"We'll discuss the other issue when I get back."

She bit her lip and nodded. It went against her instincts, he knew, to leave, but she would. Keeping her sister in Lost River was too important to mess up.

As she ran into the storm, Daryn faced the teen. "Okay. Let's talk man to man."

"You're wasting your time with me."

"Shouldn't that be my decision?"

"Why do you care?" He stuffed his hands in his pockets and hunched his shoulders. "You don't know me."

"I know you believe nobody cares what happens to you. You believe they care only about you doing what they expect you to do and when they expect it done."

The teen stared at him in disbelief. "How do you know?"

"One thing you need to learn, Perry, is what you feel isn't unique." He held up his hands to halt the boy's protest. "Don't waste your breath. I know what you're going to say. Nobody has been as misunderstood as you are. Nobody has been as underappreciated or as underestimated as you are. Nobody has worked so hard and failed so much as you have because everyone's expectations are unreasonable. Nobody has had it rougher than you have it." He gave a humorless chuckle. "I know because I've felt the same."

"But your *daed* didn't call you a loser and pack you off to live with relatives you don't know."

He held the teen's gaze, daring Perry to look away. When the boy didn't, Daryn said, "No, my *daed* didn't say that. Instead, he called himself a loser because he thought, in spite of his hard work, he'd failed to train me up as a *kind* should be. *Then* he packed me off to live with my brother." He halted Perry's retort by hurrying to say, "I know you're going to say at least I knew my brother. I knew him as my brother, not as my guardian who believed I should take his orders as if they were direct from the *Ordnung*."

"Malachi can be that way. Alberta, too. She snaps at me if I'm a second late with anything."

"All the time?"

Perry poked at the stone with his boot. "No. Just before she has to lie down."

"So when she's in pain?"

"*Ja.*"

Daryn doubted he'd ever heard a more reluctant answer. "They're trying their best. As my brother did. Mark wasn't unreasonable, but I'd gotten so accustomed to ignoring what *Daed* said it became a habit I transferred to Mark. How could I have guessed he was expending every bit of his patience while trying to guide me to a path that would make me happy and allow me to walk with God?"

"At least your brother cared."

"I didn't think so. That's how I know you don't think your *daed* cares for you."

"He doesn't. He kicked me out."

Daryn shook his head. "He didn't kick you out. He sent you to his brother, hoping you'd be happier here."

"Or he'd be happier without me." He sniffed his derision, but it sounded more like a sob. "Why would he send me to Alberta and Malachi? Did he think they were such great parents when their daughter ran away?"

"Bethany is back." He hadn't intended to tell the teen, but he had to make Perry hear what he was saying.

Perry stared at him, his mouth dropping. "Are you serious?"

"It's the truth. While they were looking for you around the farm, Carrie found her in the house." He didn't mention the *boppli*. "If you don't believe me, *komm* and see." When the boy hesitated, he added, "Perry, the past is over. You've got to think of the future. The Detweilers will stand beside you if you have to go to court." He grasped the teen's arm. "So will I."

"You will?"

"*Ja*. You won't be alone. You're not the same guy who came to Lost River. You've been working hard for the Detweilers, for Kolton and for me. The judge will take that under consideration."

"Before he locks me up?"

"He's not going to lock you up. You may have to pay a fine to cover repairs to the buildings and the food carts you vandalized."

"I didn't spray anything on Carrie's trailer. I told the guys to leave it alone, but one of them must have gone back."

"No honor among thieves, ain't so?"

"We didn't steal anything!"

"So you bought the paint?"

Perry stared at his sneakers that were splattered with every color that had been sprayed in Dashtown. "There was more than enough for that ridiculous mural. We just borrowed some."

"The judge will have to decide if he's going to buy that excuse. You may have to serve community service hours, but you won't go to jail. Not this time. Take this whole experience as a chance to learn, so you don't have to worry about going to jail the next time you mess up."

"How do you know I'm going to mess up again?"

"Because we all do. It's your choice whether you mess up big or you mess up small. Which will it be?"

Daryn held his breath. Saying anything else might tip Perry the wrong way. Backing the kid into a corner wouldn't help. It was time for Perry to decide which road he'd take.

"All right," Perry said, his arrogant pose gone. Did that mean he was willing to return to the Detweilers' and face the consequences of his vandalism in Dashtown? "I'll go back."

"*Gut* man." Daryn clapped him on the shoulder, and the teen stood a bit taller.

The trip to the Detweiler farm was different from the one he'd taken with Carrie earlier. Not only did he and Perry have to walk in the rain that thudded around them, but the teen filled every minute with talk. Daryn was grateful when Gerald appeared in a wagon and gave them a lift. Sitting in the rear and pulling his hat low over his brow as he hunched into his shirt, he closed his eyes and focused on the happiness he'd found with Carrie.

Gerald pulled the wagon to a stop near the farmhouse, and Kayla pushed open the house door. She raced across the wet lawn. Daryn jumped out, catching her before she slid.

She grabbed Daryn's hand and tugged. "*Komm mol!*" she shouted. "*Onkel* Daryn, *komm mol*. Right now!"

"What's wrong?" He wondered how such a simple question could have so many possible horrible answers.

"Ella! She won't stop crying."

"Crying?" he asked in astonishment. "Ella is crying where others can see her?"

What had driven the little girl to weep openly? That was one answer he wasn't sure he wanted to hear.

Chapter Fourteen

Carrie whirled when her parents' bedroom door opened. When she saw Daryn in the doorway, she motioned for him to hurry in. Over the soft sobbing from the bed, she whispered, "Ella was crying when I got back. She hasn't stopped."

"Is she hurt?"

Sorrow thickened in her throat so she struggled to swallow when she picked up a battered stuffed toy. It was Freckles. Had Ella tossed it aside or had it fallen off the bed unnoticed?

"Not that I can see," she managed to say.

"Has anyone else been up here?" He cut his eyes to the wall between her parents' room and the one she'd shared with Bethany. Where Bethany and her son must be sleeping deeply.

The crying hadn't woken them. She didn't want to think about what hardships they'd faced that kept a *kind*'s cry from waking her sister.

"Nobody." Her *daed* was busy tending to *Mamm*, and Gerald had made it clear he wanted nothing to do with a weeping *kind*.

Ella was rolled into a ball, shaking with sobs. The other two clung to each other.

"Let me try to calm Ella, Daryn," she murmured so her voice wouldn't carry to the *kinder* in this room or the other.

"Once she stops crying, let me know."

His dismal acceptance hurt her heart. He'd done so much to try to reach his oldest niece, but Ella had never responded. For the first time, she understood the depth of his disappointment. She'd dreamed of helping Bethany when she returned. Instead Bethany had pushed her away. Tears rose, but she blinked them away as she closed the door after Daryn had stepped into the hall. Taking a breath to steady herself, she looked at the bed.

A shiver of something primitive and cold slithered through her when Ella sat bolt upright in bed. The little girl cried so softly Carrie had to strain her ears to catch the sound. Was this how Ella always cried? If so, had she been crying when they'd thought she was asleep or paging through a book?

Edging around the younger girls, Carrie knelt on the floor. Why was Ella inconsolable? Did the *kind* have any idea how Carrie could have dissolved into tears along with her? Up until now, Ella had been strong.

Too strong.

She winced as she thought of the many times she had been unable to reach Ella. How many times she'd thought she might be more successful the next time…and failed.

Leaning toward Ella, she asked, "*Liebling*, what's wrong? Tell me, so I can help."

Kayla scrambled up on the bed between her older sister and Carrie. Crossing her arms over her tiny chest, she said, "She not talk to you."

"*Liebling*," she tried again. "Tell me—"

"No! She not talk to *you*." Tears ran down Kayla's cheeks. "*Mamm* saided not talk to liars."

"Liars?" Carrie recoiled from the rancor in the little girl's voice. "I haven't lied to you. None of you."

"Lie. Big lie."

Carrie closed her eyes as she fought to keep from dissolving into tears. First, her twin sister acted as if she didn't want to be near her. Now, a little girl she'd taken into her heart was calling her a liar. Searching her mind, she wondered what she might have said that Kayla had misconstrued. Not only Kayla, but Ella as well. Opening her eyes, she glanced at where Rae-Rae sat with two fingers in her mouth and a trail of tears on her cheeks.

"I want to help Ella," Carrie said.

"No Carrie." Kayla pointed past her at the door. "Want *Onkel* Daryn."

Joy should have swarmed through her as the little girl asked for her *onkel*, but as she pushed herself to stand, grief as strong as the morning she'd discovered her twin was gone flooded her. She'd thought she comprehended how Daryn felt each time his niece kept him away. She hadn't. The pain was worse than anything she could imagine.

"Me?" Daryn choked when Carrie opened the door and told him what Kayla had said. "Why would Ella want to talk to me? She hasn't said a single word to me tonight."

"I don't know, but Kayla said you're the one who has to try."

He looked through the doorway. The soft murmur of his nieces' voices, trying to comfort their older sister, pierced his heart. He took a step forward before he realized Carrie hadn't moved to follow. He started to lift his hand toward her, then dropped it to his side. She was giving him the opportunity to make—at long last—an abiding connection with his oldest niece. Would it be possible? He didn't know, and neither did she. For the first time since she'd given the girls French fries and books at the park, she appeared as uncertain as he was about what to do next. He was astonished to realize how much he'd been following her lead with the girls, letting her set the pace. Not that she'd put a foot wrong, but it was past time for him to build a bridge between the girls' pasts and their futures.

Walking into the room, he was shocked when Rae-Rae and Kayla threw themselves at him, hiding their faces against his legs as they wept, too. He almost looked back at Carrie, then asked himself what she'd do to reach the girls. She'd soothe them with a gentle voice and let his nieces know they were loved.

"*Komm* with me," he murmured as he put his arm around each set of tiny shoulders. Steering them to where Ella was curled into a ball as she quaked with sobs, he lifted Rae-Rae, then Kayla onto the bed and sat on its edge. They locked their arms around his, not wanting him to leave them. Leaning toward their older sister, he said, "I know it's sad." He shook his head. "No, sad is too little a word. What's inside me is like a big bad bear ripping me into teeny pieces. He's there, growling and hurting, each time I try to breathe. Every beat of my heart struggles against him because he keeps growing bigger and bigger. The part of me that's *me* is fighting to get through each day."

"Not bear," Kayla said. "Shark. Big mean blue shark."

He was startled, then remembered a book they had about the ocean. A blue-tinted shark was on the cover.

"Gots big, big, big teeth." Rae-Rae shuddered and crawled onto his lap, sticking her thumb in her mouth.

"It's not a bear or a shark." Ella's voice was a whisper. "It's a lion. It roars, and it has sharp claws."

"Not lion." Kayla shook her head. "Can't be a lion."

"Why not?" he asked.

The little girl perched on his other knee, and Rae-Rae shifted to give her room. They nestled close. "Like lions. Nice big kitties. Soft like a llama."

Daryn couldn't follow Kayla's logic as she moved from talking about one animal to another.

"Carrie gots two llamas. She…" She glanced toward her older sister as her voice faded.

Ella glowered at her. "No Carrie. She lies."

"Carrie?" He shook his head. "Carrie doesn't lie." He didn't add that, if anything, Carrie was too forthright, refusing to brush the rough edges off the truth.

"*Ja*, she does!"

"What lie do you think she's told you?"

For the first time, the little girl met his gaze without looking away. He was shoved backward by the power of agony shining in her eyes. How could such a tiny form hold so much pain without exploding? He'd been battling with his grief and succumbing more times than he wanted to count. She'd somehow managed to restrain hers behind a facade of indifference.

"Carrie's twin is back. Eli isn't."

His breath caught on the serrated blades of grief. "I know."

"But she said her twin was gone." A hiccupping sob broke her voice. "Her twin isn't gone. Her twin is here, but Eli isn't."

"She didn't lie to you, Ella. She had no idea where her twin was. Whether she was on earth or with God in Heaven."

"Eli is gone."

He gave into the silent urgings from his heart and put his arm around the little girl, drawing her up against his side.

"*Ja*, Eli is gone, but he's never completely gone as long as you remember him and love him."

"Gone. Eli all gone." New sobs exploded from her. She pulled away from Daryn and slid off the bed. Taking a single step, she collapsed to the floor with a thud that sent a renewed resonance of pain through him. Unable to move because of the two little girls on his lap, he watched as Carrie stepped forward and knelt beside the huddled *kind*.

When Carrie scooped her up, nobody spoke. Ella's sobs became gentle hiccups, then little gasps. Was she regaining her composure or running out of tears?

He got his answer when she turned in Carrie's arms so she could see him and her sisters.

"Sorry, Kayla. Sorry, Rae-Rae," she said in a raw voice.

Carrie caught his eyes over the little girl's head and mouthed, *Talk to her. Don't stop.*

As he had so many times since his nieces had arrived at the ranch, he prayed for God to give him the words to show how much he loved these three precious little girls. How he'd loved them before he'd met them because Hope had made them *komm* to life in her letters. "What are you sorry about, Ella?"

"Making Kayla and Rae-Rae sad." Another wave of tears threatened to spill from her eyes that were the same bright blue as his. "I didn't want to…" She seemed unable to find words to explain.

But he thought he understood. Squatting so he was eye-to-eye with Ella, he said, "You're a brave and *wunderbaar* little girl, Ella. You worried about your sisters and wanted to keep them from hurting more, ain't so? They're blessed to have you in their lives."

"I didn't want them to be sadder."

"I know." He wiped away one of her tears with his

crooked finger. "I know because I tried to do the same. I thought if I hid how sad I was that you'd be happier."

"You did?"

"You did?" echoed her sisters in near unison.

He gave each a gentle smile. "*Ja*, I did."

"I thought you didn't care." Ella met his gaze in her uncompromising way that reminded him so much of his sister.

Her simple words were like a heated knife in his heart. "I cared, Ella. There aren't words to tell you how much I cared. I loved my sister, though she sometimes annoyed me. She used to hide my toys when I was little, and she wouldn't give them back unless I let her have my share of the cookies *Mamm*—your *grossmammi*—had given us."

"*Mamm*... My *mamm* did that?" she asked as her sisters climbed from the bed to flank her. To bolster her or protect her as she'd protected them?

"*Ja*, but she was also the one who held my hand on the first day I went to school and let me sit at her desk until I was brave enough to join the other first graders at the front of the room. I loved your *mamm*. I will love her every day of my life." He grasped their small hands. "As I love each of you."

When Ella and Kayla burst into tears, Rae-Rae gasped and turned to him.

"It's okay to be sad," he said.

"It is?" Rae-Rae looked from him to Carrie who was rocking her sisters. "No cry. They said no cry."

He didn't bother to ask who *they* were. Someone with *gut* intentions or whose heart had been torn apart by the sight of three orphans whose life had been upended. Had the words been before the funeral or after? How many people had uttered them, hoping to bring the girls comfort?

"There's a lesson I should have learned when I was your age, Rae-Rae," he said, but all the *kinder* were looking at him. "It's taken me years to learn it. I don't want you to have to wait so long to understand what's true."

"What?" asked Kayla.

"You have to learn *they* are never as *gut* a source of information as God. He is in your heart, and He's the one to listen to because He knows all that has been, what is and what will be. If I had heeded Him more and others less, I would have saved myself a lot of trouble." He touched the center of Kayla's chest. "What does your heart tell you?"

The little girl didn't answer right away. She gave his question more thought than he'd expected, because Kayla had always been the first to respond to everything. She must have been more changed by her grief than he'd imagined. He asked himself why the little girl should be different from him. Grief had rewritten every cell in his body, more than once, changing him from a *gut* kid to a troubled one to a man who longed to remake his life into something that wouldn't cause his family pain or shame.

"God makes me, ain't so?" Kayla asked as she inched closer to him and her little sister.

"*Ja.*" He wasn't sure where she was going with her question.

"He makes my fingers and my toes, ain't so?"

"*Ja.*" Sensing Carrie's gaze on them, he shifted his eyes toward her.

She rose, holding Ella, and came to sit on the bed beside him. The younger girls hurried to join them. Not saying a word, she gave Kayla an encouraging smile as she wrapped an arm around the little girl's shoulders.

It was what the *kind* needed to continue with more assurance. "God makes my fingers and Rae-Rae's toes and Ella's mouth and Daryn's and Carrie's noses." She giggled at her rhyme. "Toes and noses."

He tapped her foot and then her nose. "*Ja*, God made our toes and noses. He brought each of us to life and—"

"He makes everybody's tears." She touched her cheek where stains marked where hers had flowed. "He gives us tears. Happy tears. Sad tears. Glad tears. Mad tears." She laughed. "Sad. Glad. Mad. That's fun to say, ain't so?"

"*Ja*, it is." He stood and picked up Kayla. "But none of you will be fun tomorrow if you don't get sleep tonight." Putting the little girl on the bed, he lifted her sisters beside her. "Under the covers."

He listened while they said their prayers as if it was their regular bedtime. Carrie handed the battered toy to Ella, who drew it close. She bent to kiss each of his nieces on the forehead before stepping aside to let him do the same. Ella threw her arms around his neck, holding him close for only a moment before snuggling into the mattress and closing her eyes. Her sisters followed suit.

Daryn watched them, thanking God for opening their hearts to let him in. He was reluctant to leave, but did. His happiness tempered when he saw Carrie staring at the closed door on the next room. It must be where her sister and her nephew were sleeping. She glanced at him, then hurried to the empty living room. He wasn't sure where her parents were while his nieces slept in their bed. Exhaustion and emotion overwhelmed him.

"You can use the sofa," she whispered with a fake smile.

"And you?"

"I'm not tired." She didn't meet his eyes.

"You told Ella you don't lie, so why are you being false with me? You're weaving on your feet after a long day of cooking in Dashtown and chasing after your cousin and having Beth—"

She held up her hand. "She doesn't want everyone to know she's here."

"It's only a few hours until dawn. You can't keep her hidden forever. Tomorrow is coming, whether we want it to or not. Tomorrow, everything is going to be different. I've got to find a way to keep Ella talking to me. She may have given me a hug, but her heart is broken. We need to find ways to help heal my family as well as yours."

Shaking her head, she crossed the room. He followed, not wanting to raise his voice above a whisper and complicate the conversation by having her parents or brother or cousin appear and discover what they were discussing.

She faced him, her feigned smile gone. "You're asking the wrong person. I was arrogant enough to think I could help you. The truth is I can't help myself." Tears bubbled from her eyes, astonishing him.

Footsteps sounded upstairs. Not from her parents' room, so he guessed they belonged to her sister. When Carrie wrapped her arms around herself and seemed to shrink, he grasped her shoulders. "God has granted you your most precious wish. Are you going to toss that gift away because it's not what you thought it would be?"

"I don't know."

He was astonished. He'd thought Carrie wouldn't have been able to wait a second longer to spend time with her sister and her nephew. Despite what she'd said about Bethany pushing her away, he knew Carrie. She was persistent when she believed someone needed her help. He'd seen multiple examples of that himself, so what had changed?

Taking her hands, he said, "You can't run away from a problem, Carrie. I know. I've tried it over and over, and it hasn't worked. Not once."

"You said that to Perry."

"I did. I used to think I was smart when I decided the way to deal with problems was to run away. It took years for me to learn how stupid that is. I don't want to see him— or you—suffering the same long years of loss and pain." He paused and glanced up the stairs when he heard a soft female voice. Her twin sister was talking to her son in the same gentle, loving tone Carrie used with his nieces.

She'd given him and the girls so much by showing it was okay to smile when days were at their darkest.

Something he hadn't been able to do, letting himself forget how to smile.

She hadn't hesitated to go after her dreams in spite of every obstacle.

He'd seen what he wanted as an escape, not as a goal.

Most important, she'd dared to dream.

Something he'd found difficult to do after his mistakes caught up with him. He'd convinced himself he didn't deserve happiness, and he'd begun to believe it until tragedy brought into his life three adorable little girls who didn't care if he had a smudged past or not. All they cared was that he loved them.

He'd been given a second chance to change his life, and Carrie had led him to see that with her unfailing optimism. If he'd let his pessimism overshadow her joy, it was the worst mistake he'd made, and it was one mistake he wasn't going to run away from.

"Go and talk to her, Carrie."

"She told me—"

"*Ja.* I know she told you what she feels, but did you tell her how you feel?" When her eyes widened, he pressed his point. "You need to be honest with her."

"I don't know what to say."

"I think you do." He put his hands on her shoulders,

pleased at how close she was in height to him. He kept talk-ing so he didn't kiss her as he yearned to. "You have a way of sensing what another person needs to hear. Not always what they want to hear, but what they *must* hear."

She didn't lower her gaze, and he made no effort to hide how much he admired her quiet strength and how she didn't play games.

"Go before it's too late," he urged, then held his breath, hoping she'd let him help her as she'd helped him.

Carrie stopped in front of the bedroom door, wanting to chicken out. Aware of how Daryn waited downstairs, ex-pecting her to be brave enough to face her fear of sending her sister fleeing by saying the wrong thing, she opened the door and walked in. She prayed God would guide her steps and her mouth.

Bethany was watching her son, who was lying on the bed that had been hers for as long as Carrie could remem-ber. She wore an off-putting scowl that Daryn would have envied when he was at his grimmest.

"Carrie, can't this wait until morning?" she asked coolly.

"No."

Her sister's expression went from surprise to resignation. "So you can't wait to give me the third degree?"

"I'm not going to do that."

"*Mamm* and *Daed* will."

Carrie almost said how worried her parents had been about their missing daughter, so worried that *Mamm*'s head-aches had increased in strength and frequency. She halted herself. "Gerald will be the worst. Do you want to know how I know that?" Not giving her sister time to answer, she said, "Because for the past two years, I haven't stepped a toe outside this house without him asking where I'm going, how long I'll be gone and if I'll be with anyone. If he doesn't like my answers, he keeps pushing until I start to wonder if it would be easier to stay home." She let a smile tip her lips. "But I don't because I don't want him to think he can browbeat me."

"You were always the strongest of us." Bethany sighed and sat beside her son who remained asleep. "If I'd had half your strength and clear view of what's right and what's not, my life might have been different. I guess I owe you for putting up with Gerald. So what do you want to know?"

Dozens of questions vied to be asked first. Questions of why Bethany had left and where she'd been and what had happened to Aidan's *daed*. What had convinced Bethany to leave with Mike Houlihan? Had she been pregnant when she'd fled from Lost River? Her sister had avoided saying exactly how old her son was. Those questions billowed through her head, but only one had to be spoken.

"Why didn't you leave me a message the night you left?" Carrie asked as she sat on her bed, far enough away so she didn't crowd her sister.

Bethany's eyes widened, and Carrie guessed her question hadn't been the one her twin expected her to ask first. It wasn't the question she'd intended, but it was the one that had burst forth from the most pain-flooded part of her heart. She almost reached for her sister's hands. She didn't, not wanting Bethany to pull away.

Quiet settled on the room, making the tick from the alarm clock seem preternaturally loud. Its rhythm was slower than Carrie's frantic heartbeat as she waited for her sister's response.

When it came, Bethany's voice sounded, for the first time since she'd returned, like the one Carrie remembered instead of the robotic tone she'd used as if she'd practiced what she would say over and over.

"I meant to leave you a note, Carrie, but I didn't have time. That was the night we had our quilting circle, and the horse pulled up lame on our way home."

"I remember. We had to walk. We were an hour late getting home."

Bethany nodded, pulling her legs up so she could wrap her arms around her knees as if they were young teens, sitting in their room and sharing confidences and discussing dreams. "I had to be ready to leave minutes after we got in."

"You must have been already packed."

"I was. Mostly." She glanced at where her son slept with the small stuffed bear in his arms. "I couldn't leave Patches behind."

"Because you knew you were pregnant?"

Bethany looked at her. "I suspected I was. I hadn't seen a *doktor*, and I didn't dare to get a pregnancy test to confirm my suspicions." She shivered. "I knew if I stayed much longer, *Mamm* or one of the other women would guess the truth. As it was, I had to hide my morning sickness. If *Mamm* had been at the table for every meal instead of helping one of the neighbors—I don't remember which one—she would have seen how much I ate. Everything I smelled made me feel nauseated." A weary smile returned to her face. "Patches belongs to my son. He won't go to sleep without it."

"But if you came up here to get Patches, why didn't you leave me a note to tell me where you were going?"

"Because I didn't know where Mike and I were headed."

"What happened to Mike?"

"He died while trying to save someone else's life." She held up her hands to forestall Carrie's next question. "He was a *gut* man, Carrie. He loved me, and he loved Aidan.

That's why I knew when I met him that he was the one God wanted me to be with. God walked with me the night we left, and He's been with me every step of the way. I trusted Him, and I trusted Mike when he said it'd be better I didn't know too much in case we were stopped." She shook her head as Carrie began to protest that nobody would have grilled them if they happened to see her sister and the *Englischer* on the street. "You know that's not true. You would have been the first to ask me."

"I missed you," she whispered, unable to keep the truth inside her any longer.

Bethany shuddered as Ella had when the little girl tried to hold in her pain. "I missed you, too, Carrie. More than I could explain."

When Carrie wrapped her arms around her twin sister, she felt whole, something she hadn't been in two years. Then she realized as her sister hugged her that her heart was more than whole. It was overflowing with love.

She released her sister. Telling Bethany to rest and that she'd do her best to keep her presence a secret until Bethany and Aidan woke, she slid off the bed and from the room. She tiptoed down the stairs to where Daryn was waiting for her…as she'd known he would.

Happiness—true happiness, not the mask she'd created for the past two years—bubbled within her like a mountain spring awakening after a long and cold winter. She glided across the room to where she slipped her arms around his broad shoulders.

Smiling at the shock in his blue eyes, she said, "*Danki*, Daryn. I guess when I believed Bethany was lost, I got lost too. I spent so much time stuck in one moment—the one when I discovered she was gone and I was alone—that I didn't know how to escape from my grief and blame."

"Blame?" His arms curved around her waist, holding her close to him.

"*Ja.* I never said anything, but I felt it was my fault she left. We'd always shared everything."

"Or so you thought."

"Or so I thought," she repeated. "I couldn't imagine any reason why she'd want to leave unless I'd done something wrong and pushed her away. I know it doesn't make sense, but it's what was in the depths of my heart."

"No, it makes a lot of sense because I was doing pretty much the same thing except I was blaming everyone *but* myself for the distance that grew between me and my family. Not just the miles, but the distance between our hearts. I convinced myself if I kept everyone away, they wouldn't ask about why I'd left my family."

"I wanted to be happy and sunny so nobody could guess there was dark pain inside me."

"I was spending every day trying to be as grim as possible so nobody would get close enough to see how I missed smiling and laughing and the joy of being around those I care about. Those I love."

"You smile. Occasionally."

He did, but sadness clung to his eyes. "While you frown. Occasionally. I miss your smile every time it disappears." As his hand curved along her cheek, she was torn. She wanted to close her eyes and savor the touch of his work-hardened hands. At the same time, she didn't want to tear her eyes away from his gaze. "*Ich liebe dich*, Carrie. I can't remember a time when I didn't love you."

"That's ridiculous." Her giggle sounded as young and carefree as Kayla's. "You've known me only a year or so."

"Maybe, but you are the one I've been seeking my whole life. Someone who accepts me as I am. Someone who knows

I'm going to mess up, but I'm trying to do my best. Someone who believed in my dreams when I didn't and the possibility I could become the man I wanted to be."

"A man with three nieces and a herd of bison?"

"That's the dream, though you left out one important part. A wife. You. Will you marry me, *liebling*? Make me into a man who can't stop smiling."

"*Ja*." She met his lips with her eager ones, savoring their touch, which sent sunlight to the darkest crevices of her heart.

Epilogue

The autumn breeze made the curtains on the temporary building flap, but nobody paid them any attention. The wedding pavilion, a large modular building with more windows and doors than walls, had been erected in the Detweilers' front yard. From it, guests saw curious llamas wondering why so many humans had gathered on a Tuesday in late September.

Daryn shrugged on his *mutze* coat, brushing invisible lint from its front. As he hooked it closed, a motion outside the window caught his eye. He smiled when he saw Josiah Reimer doing last-minute checks on the building he'd brought and set-up last night. It was a new business for the widower who was, according to Kolton, seeking ways to fill his days since his wife had died last year.

Josiah was one of the firefighters Daryn had met since he'd begun training with the Lost River Volunteer Fire Department. The volunteers—*Englisch* and plain—were a close-knit community, and they'd welcomed him and Carrie like long-lost family.

At that thought, he listened to the footsteps upstairs. Carrie was getting ready with the so-called help of his nieces. They were too young to serve as *Newehockers*, the attendants to the groom and his bride, but she wanted to include them in the wedding. Their dresses today were small copies of the light blue dress with a white organdy apron to match the ones Carrie wore.

"Looks like you've found where you belong."

Daryn heard his brother's relief as Mark walked into the living room. A few years ago, Daryn would have assumed his brother was trying to run his life by stating the obvious. He understood now the words showcased how glad Mark was that Daryn had given up searching for a place he could call home. Daryn had stopped chasing it long enough to let it settle around him. As Mark had, Daryn realized. Mark had moved from Ontario to Prince Edward Island to seek the life he wanted. He'd risked everything he had to get all he wanted.

As Daryn had.

While it had taken Mark a single move, Daryn had traveled a more convoluted journey to happiness.

Mark clapped him on the shoulder, but said nothing more. There was nothing else that needed to be said. Daryn knew his brother had forgiven him for the trouble he'd caused, and Daryn had forgiven his brother for trying to be the parent Daryn had believed he no longer needed.

Like his brother, he'd had parenthood thrust upon him. He'd made mistakes as Mark had, but he appreciated all his brother had done for him. Mark had been touched when Daryn sought his advice for raising their nieces. A few questions closed the chasm Daryn had dug between them.

Ella, Kayla and Rae-Rae half ran, half stumbled down the stairs. Kayla skipped over to him, asking, "Ride Monty today?" Her hair was already escaping her braids.

His former boss had insisted Monty go with Daryn when he bought an abandoned farm near the county line to the east. "The girls will need to learn to ride if they're going to help you with those overgrown cows." Carlos's laugh had boomed through the afternoon air.

With the help of friends and Carrie's family, they'd begun the work on the ramshackle house and barn and outbuildings. It would be years before the renovations were completed, but enough had been done so the house was habitable and there was shelter for Monty, the other horses and the four bison cows he'd bought for the beginnings of his herd.

"Monty has today off to celebrate," Daryn said. "How about tomorrow?"

With that to look forward to, his nieces went with his brother to take their seats in the wedding pavilion where the *Leit* waited. Jerek and the other ordained men came into the house for the pre-wedding counseling. It was the final step before the wedding could happen. As they sat in the comfortable living room, the sound of singing came from the pavilion. It would continue until the bride and groom entered together.

From the other side of the room, Perry gave Daryn a thumbs-up. The teen had accepted his punishment of community service for his vandalism in Dashtown. Since then, he'd found better friends and an apprenticeship with Leon whose blacksmithy wasn't far from the Detweiler farm. He'd selected a youth group where several of the girls—at least according to Perry—were interested in him. Exactly what a normal teen boy should think.

Wondering how he could be any happier, Daryn got his answer when Carrie joined them. Her golden hair gleamed beneath her white *kapp*, and her eyes glowed with love as they met his. As he sat beside her on the sofa, he didn't hear anything Jerek said, echoing Carrie's answers to their bishop. His thoughts were filled with gratitude that this *wunderbaar* woman would be his for the rest of their lives.

The men stood and left to join the others in the pavilion. Coming to his feet, Daryn offered his hand to Carrie. She placed hers on it. He drew her into his arms. Her response to his swift kiss was one he knew wouldn't lessen no matter how often he kissed her.

"Are you ready to marry Grumpy?" he asked with a grin.

Her eyes widened. "You know about Paige's nickname for you?"

"I know lots you don't know I know."

In the same teasing voice, she said, "Well, I've got a lifetime to discover those secrets, ain't so?"

With a laugh and another kiss, they headed into their future, which would be filled with sunshine and shadows which they would get through together.

* * * * *

*If you enjoyed this story, don't miss these other books
from Jo Ann Brown in the
Amish of Lost River miniseries:*

Healing Her Amish Heart
Saving Her Amish Baby
Their Amish Courtship Secret

Find more great reads at www.LoveInspired.com

Dear Reader,

Welcome back…or welcome to the San Luis Valley in Colorado! It's so easy to see someone for the first time and make assumptions about them. We see a welcoming smile or a distancing glower and judge a person instantly. Just human nature, isn't it? Or "ain't so?" as my Amish neighbors would say. Both Carrie and Daryn need to look past first impressions to find a lasting impression…and isn't it fun to be surprised by someone who may, even after a not-so-great first encounter, become a dear, dear friend?

Visit me at www.joannbrownbooks.com. And look for my next book in the *Amish of Lost River* series coming soon!

Wishing you many blessings,
Jo Ann Brown